THE MINDEN CURSE

THE MINDEN CURSE

WILLO DAVIS ROBERTS

Aladdin Books
Macmillan Publishing Company
New York

First Aladdin Books edition 1990

Aladdin Books
Macmillan Publishing Company
866 Third Avenue, New York, NY 10022
Collier Macmillan Canada, Inc.

Printed in the United States of America

A hardcover edition of *The Minden Curse* is available from
Atheneum Publishers, Macmillan Publishing Company.

10   9   8   7   6   5   4   3   2   1

Library of Congress Cataloging-in-Publication Data

Roberts, Willo Davis.
    The minden curse / Willo Davis Roberts.—1st Aladdin Books ed.
        p.   cm.
    Summary: When Danny goes to a small village to live with his aunt
and grandfather, it soon becomes apparent that he and his dog are
afflicted with the Minden Curse: Whenever catastrophes occur, they're
sure to be involved.
    ISBN 0-689-71378-9 (pbk.)
    [1. Mystery and detective stories.]   I. Title.
PZ7.R54465Mi   1990
[Fic]—dc20   89-18336   CIP   AC

1

It wasn't my idea to go to Indian Lake for a year. I'd been there when I was a little kid, for Christmas a couple of times and once for Thanksgiving. Aunt Mattie's a good cook, and once I ate so much turkey I thought I'd die. But as far as I could see there was nothing to do there except eat.

I'd been there about six hours this time, and so far that's all I'd done. Eat. Chicken and dumplings, which I had to admit were great and were something Dad and I didn't get very often in hotels.

And there was Leroy. I hadn't expected to find him, because the last time I'd been there they had a big black cat named Stoney, but Stoney had died since then.

Leroy was the biggest dog I'd ever seen in my life. The biggest, and the homeliest. There was no kind way to describe that dog: he had to be the epitome of ugly. Epitome means *the most*.

When I saw Leroy I said a word my dad sometimes says when he's surprised, and Gramps looked at me over his glasses. Gramps was sort of skinny, and he had white hair and blue eyes so faded they were pale blue, but when he looked at you, it was for sure he really saw you. Even inside, what you were thinking sometimes. "I wouldn't use words like that around your Aunt Mattie. Women are funny about such things."

"Sorry. I forgot. What is he?"

"He's a dog. Name of Leroy."

"Is he ours? I mean, yours?"

"I don't reckon he's anybody's, but I've been feeding him the past week or so. Looked like he could use a meal."

He wasn't very fat yet. "Are you going to keep him?" I asked hopefully. I didn't care about getting acquainted with those peers my dad kept talking about, but I'd always wanted a dog. It was one of the things you couldn't have when you traveled all the time.

"Well, that's something Mattie and I haven't yet agreed upon," Gramps said. "She says he'll cost a fortune to feed, and no doubt she's right."

"He looks like an Irish wolfhound," I said, and for just a second I thought about my dad, who'd soon be on his way to Ireland. "Dad took pictures at a dog show once, and they had Irish wolfhounds. Only they didn't look quite so—"

"Tacky?" Gramps suggested, grinning. "Well, I suspect Leroy has a few other strains in his ancestry, too. But the size is wolfhound, all right. Leroy, this is Danny. He's going to be living with us until school is out next spring."

I found out Gramps always talked to Leroy like that, as if he were a person. And not just Leroy, but any animal. Even ladybugs.

So after supper I talked to him, too. "You want to go for a walk, Leroy?"

The dog looked at me with gentle eyes and wagged a shaggy tail. He was shaggy all over, actually, and sort of salt-and-pepper colored. More pepper than salt, so he came out grayish.

"OK, come on," I invited, and he followed me down the steps.

The back door was really the front door at Aunt Mattie's house. That is, it faced the road. The fronts of all the houses faced the lake. It wasn't a big lake, but it was a nice one.

We went down to the edge of it and I felt the water, which was sort of milky-blue in the fading light. It was warm, warm enough to swim in. Maybe I'd do that tomorrow, I thought.

I kicked at a log and then sat down on it and wrote

words in the sand between my feet. Bad words. Words nobody would let me say to express how I felt about coming here.

Leroy leaned against me, and when I turned my head he licked my face. He was so huge he could do it sitting down.

"You been kicked around, too?" I asked him. "People make you do things you don't want to do?"

Leroy wagged his tail. I guess he felt sympathetic toward me, even if he didn't understand what my problem was. Well, if I didn't make any friends here, I'd have Leroy to talk to.

It wasn't completely satisfying, though. He was friendly, but he didn't answer back. He'd go exploring with me, I supposed, though I wasn't very optimistic about what there was to explore. A bunch of summer houses around the lake, most of them empty now because the people all went back to the cities by Labor Day. Beyond them there were woods. Maybe there'd be something interesting in the woods, though I doubted it.

I just sat there on the log, feeling sorry for myself and scratching Leroy behind the ears. The water turned black in the twilight and then lights came on in the two places beyond ours that were still inhabited, and it got so dark I couldn't have found our own house if the lights hadn't been on.

I swatted a mosquito that landed on my neck. I

heard Aunt Mattie call to me, but I pretended I didn't hear her. I didn't want to go back inside; I hadn't wanted to come here, and I didn't want to give in and become part of a new family and start fitting into their routine. Dad and I had got along all right for seven years, ever since my mom died when I was four, so why did everything have to be spoiled now?

Leroy finally leaned so hard he shoved me right off the log; and when I stood up, I saw the lights.

"You big dumb—" I was saying, but I stopped, because according to Aunt Mattie there wasn't anybody living out on that part of the lake, at the end of our road.

There were lights, though.

I wasn't very curious at first, because all I was thinking about was myself and how much I was going to hate going to school here; I was even making up wild reasons why it wouldn't work out and I could join Dad again. Like the house would burn down and there'd be nowhere to live. Only that was mean, because then Aunt Mattie and Gramps wouldn't have anywhere to live, either, so I felt guilty thinking that.

After a while I realized the lights I was seeing weren't in a house, they were flashlights, moving around. I wondered without caring very much what two people were doing with flashlights down there when all the houses were empty.

Dumb, boring lights. Dumb, boring town. Dumb,

boring people, too, I'd bet.

I kicked the sand again, and then when I heard Aunt Mattie's voice, I gave up and went back to the house.

It was in the morning that I first heard about the Minden Curse.

We had pancakes for breakfast. Big, fluffy ones, with lots of real butter and maple syrup on them. I was eating mine when Gramps came downstairs. Aunt Mattie came toward him with a plate in one hand and said, "Well, something finally happened around here that you weren't in on, Dad."

"Oh? What's that?" He fixed his pancakes, and he didn't seem upset about missing anything.

"Somebody tried to get into the Bernard place last night." She explained for my benefit: "The Bernards are an elderly couple, have a place down the lake. Come all the way from New York to spend their summers here, but by the middle of August they pack up and go to their daughter's in Portland for a month, and then back to New York. Aggie Kirk saw some mysterious lights and called the sheriff, and he went out and investigated. Sure enough, someone had pried the shutters off one window and been inside the house. I'd like to think it means the Minden Curse isn't working anymore."

"What's the Minden Curse?" I demanded. It sounded more interesting than anything they'd talked about so far, except maybe Leroy.

Gramps laughed. "You mean your dad never told you about my curse? At least that's what Mattie calls it. Keeps life from getting dull, I think, but Mattie thinks of it as an affliction."

I looked from one to the other of them, further intrigued. "So what is it? You mean there's a curse on you?"

Aunt Mattie had a peculiar expression on her face. "If anything happens in this town, Dad's always there. This is the first thing he's missed seeing in years."

I looked at Gramps with new respect. "Is that right? What sort of things?"

"Accidents, fires, you name it," Gramps said. "Last thing was the day the Mayor's wife was decorating the church for a wedding and she fell off a ladder and broke her leg. Good thing I was there to go for help. Maybe I am losing my touch, Mattie. Don't know how I missed those lights last night. Maybe they weren't anything interesting after all." He looked at me and winked.

I was beginning to have a funny feeling. Something must have showed on my face because Aunt Mattie explained some more. "Most of the people fasten shutters over their windows when they leave and lock everything up tight through the winter." Aunt Mattie had a round face and glasses she was always misplacing. She looked at me through them now and wiped a hand on her apron.

7

"I saw some lights last night," I said.

Then they both looked at me.

"You did?" Aunt Mattie asked. She didn't sound pleased at all.

"It looked like two people with flashlights, somewhere down the lake. About where that gigantic cedar tree sticks up. I remember noticing that before it got dark."

Gramps chuckled. "By golly, I think the boy's got it, too! Wouldn't that be something? Maybe he wasn't right on the spot, but he must have seen the ones who broke in! There's where the Bernard place is, all right."

Aunt Mattie pushed her glasses up on her nose and looked at me almost suspiciously, as if there was something odd about my having seen the lights. "Do you wind up in the middle of everything exciting that happens, the way Dad does?"

"Not that I know of." If I did, I'd never have wound up *here*, I thought. I'd be going to Ireland with my dad. "But I did see some lights. Did they take anything?"

"Not that Aggie or the sheriff could tell. But there'd been somebody in there, all right. What do you suppose they wanted?"

Gramps speared a sausage and bit the end off it. "Maybe it was kids fooling around."

"Maybe," Aunt Mattie said, but she didn't sound convinced.

I didn't want to be convinced it was something that simple, either. It would be neat if there was a mystery to solve; it would give me something to do.

I sort of thought about walking down there, to the Bernard house, but Aunt Mattie said I should get "settled in." That meant unpacking my stuff and putting it away in the downstairs bedroom they'd turned over to me.

She hung around and told me which drawers would be most convenient for my underwear, and where the towels were, and where the food was. That kind of thing. I wished she'd go away and leave me alone, because I halfway felt like crying and I didn't welcome the company.

"For pete's sake, Mattie, let the boy be," Gramps said finally. He was sitting in a rocking chair in the kitchen, carving something out of a chunk of wood. "He's going to be here until school's out next spring; he doesn't have to learn everything the first day, does he?"

Aunt Matti flushed. She's a nice woman, my dad's sister, but she's nothing like my mother was. Not that I remember my mother very well, because she died so long ago, but Dad carries a picture of her in his suitcase and the first thing he does when we get to a new hotel is set it out on the nightstand so we can see it.

My mother was pretty. Aunt Mattie's not homely, exactly, but she's sort of plain. Once I said maybe that was why she never got married, and Dad really read me off. Like, "People don't marry just the beauties of this world, son. Look around you. How many of us would qualify as beautiful people? You marry someone because they're good inside, and they make *you* feel good, too. And because you're friends and you like to be together. Mattie just never found the right man, I guess. But don't you downgrade her because she doesn't look like a movie star."

I didn't care what she looked like, but she made me nervous, hanging around and telling me things that were obvious. If it hadn't been for Gramps she'd have driven me crazy.

I guess that's why he rescued me.

"Leave him be," he said again, and Aunt Mattie nodded.

"I guess I'm so anxious to make Danny feel at home that I'm overdoing it."

"You are," Gramps confirmed. "Let him look around on his own, wander out in the woods or go down by the lake. Get used to us gradual."

"Gradually," Aunt Mattie corrected. She used to be a schoolteacher.

Gramps grunted. "You want to poke around on your own, boy, or would you like a guide?"

All I really wanted was to be where my dad was, but he'd told me to be polite, so I couldn't say so. "Sure, I guess a guided tour would be a good idea.

Get me oriented."

Aunt Mattie laughed. "You use some big words for a boy your age."

"That's what we always do in a new place," I told her. "Get oriented. Find out where everything is."

"Well, there's not much in Indian Lake to locate," Gramps said, putting aside his carving. I saw what it was, then, a cage with little crossbars between the up-and-down bars.

"What's that for?" I asked.

"That's for my bird," Gramps replied.

I looked around the kitchen. It was almost like a living room, because it had two rocking chairs and a window seat with a flowered cushion on it and lots of plants and books. But I didn't see any bird, and besides, it was an awfully small cage.

"What kind of bird?"

"I don't know. I haven't carved it yet," the old man said. He hitched up his suspenders so they felt comfortable. "Let's go. Maybe that old hound dog is around and will go with us."

"You're going to carve a bird to go in it? How are you going to get it inside?" I wanted to know.

"I'll carve it out of the wood that's still in there." He winked at me, and I didn't know if he was kidding or not.

"It's too bad they delayed the opening of the school for two weeks," Aunt Mattie said. "The summer kids have gone home. With me being too busy to take you around and introduce you, it will be hard to meet the other ones before school opens."

I didn't care if they delayed the opening of school permanently, and I'd gotten along all right for eleven years without meeting a bunch of kids so I thought I'd survive awhile longer. I was curious why the delay, though. Just so I wouldn't appear too ignorant when I actually got there.

"They passed a bond issue last spring, to replace all the plumbing fixtures at the school," Aunt Mattie said. "It was supposed to be done by the middle of August, and they tore out all the old fixtures. And then the new things didn't come until two days ago. My, Mr. Pepper was angry. He said they couldn't operate without rest rooms and drinking fountains. Mr. Pepper's the principal. You'll like him, Danny."

I doubted it, but I didn't say so. I just hoped that school starting late didn't mean we'd have to go half of next summer to catch up.

"You want to walk into town, then, see what it's like?" Gramps asked. "Maybe we'll see some of the kids I can introduce you to. The Hopes are still here, the last of the summer people—that's their house, the big one on down the lake. That girl of theirs is about your age, I think."

I wasn't interested in meeting any girl. I wasn't anxious to meet any boys, either.

Gramps didn't seem to notice my lack of enthusi-asm. We walked out to the road, with Leroy trotting beside me, and headed toward Indian Lake. We could see the lake between the trees, and I had to admit it was pretty, all blue and calm between the birch and cedar trees. (I could recognize some trees, even if I had never lived in the country, because my dad did an article on trees once, and I helped sort and label the pictures.)

"The Fowlers are our closest neighbors," Gramps said. "They have that little cottage between us and the Hopes. Nice young couple. Going to spend the winter, too, I guess. I hope they're going to put in some insulation or they'll freeze to death."

It was warm and sunny, and the dusty road stretched ahead of us. Things smelled good, and I relaxed and matched Gramps's pace, with Leroy touching me every so often, as if he liked to do it. I hoped Aunt Mattie was going to let him stay, even if he did eat a lot.

Gramps had been walking slowly, but all of a sud-den he started to go faster. I didn't see any reason for it, but it didn't matter to me. I speeded up, too. Leroy kept right up with us.

Gramps didn't talk much, so I had plenty of time to think. I supposed I ought to find something good about being here, something to like about Indian Lake.

The best thing would be if there was a real mystery

about those lights, but that was probably too much to hope for. Just somebody breaking in to steal something, and then they didn't find anything. Still, it was the best possibility so far. First chance I got, I'd go down there and look around. For clues, like footprints and all that stuff.

The town of Indian Lake only has about two thousand people, the sign said. There was one main street that curved along the edge of the lake and then a few streets that had just houses on them. You could see practically the whole town right from the edge of it. There was only one school; Gramps said the high school part was upstairs, and the grade school part was downstairs. I couldn't see that going there was going to be any big deal; I'd been learning all right the way I was, with just Dad for a teacher.

Once we got to town, the streets were paved, but there weren't any traffic lights except one right in the middle of town. That was because the main highway went through town, and some days, Gramps said, they'd never be able to get across the street if it wasn't for the light. Tourists, mostly, he said. I got the impression he didn't think too much of tourists.

But we didn't go down to the light to cross the street. Gramps just stepped out and moved fast, and it was a good thing he did. Because when we got to the other side, a small delivery truck came along at the same time as a sports car was pulling out of a parking spot, and they ran into each other.

It made quite a lot of noise. People started coming from everywhere to look at the damage. We didn't have to go anywhere, because it happened practically right where we were standing.

The sports car had a crumpled-up fender. Gramps opened the door and peered in at the young man at the wheel. "You all right, Jerry?"

The driver was feeling a purple lump on his forehead. "I guess so, Mr. Minden. How badly is my car smashed up?"

He got out and came around to the front, still touching his head. He was wearing ragged tennis shoes and old jeans and a sweatshirt that said "Indian Lake High" on the front of it. "Oh, wow," he said when he saw the fender.

The man who was driving the delivery truck got out and joined us. He didn't seem to have any bruises, and there was only a broken headlight on his truck.

"Holy cow, I'm sorry, Mr. Fowler! You just pulled right out in front of me. Didn't you see me coming?"

"Yes, but I thought you'd stop at the intersection," Jerry Fowler said. He had brown hair that looked as if he forgot to comb it, and he ran a hand through it and made it look even worse. "How come you didn't stop?"

Gramps answered for the truck driver. "They took out the stop signs yesterday. Didn't you know? Don't have to stop there anymore."

They talked about the damage, and Jerry Fowler bent his fender enough so he could drive his car, and we went on our way. Leroy had sat patiently waiting for us on the sidewalk; he heaved a sigh when we started out again.

I figured I'd just seen my first example of the Minden Curse, and I hoped maybe it *would* rub off on me the way Gramps said. Maybe it already had: I was there, too, when the accident happened, wasn't I? It wasn't all that exciting, only a fender-bender thing, but maybe if the Curse was catching—or hereditary—I'd find something when I went down to the Bernard place. Maybe I'd even catch some crooks.

Gramps showed me the town of Indian Lake in about half an hour. No kidding, that's all there was to see. Not even a movie theater or a bowling alley, although there was a pool hall, but Gramps said you had to be fifteen to be allowed in there. Dad taught me to play pool and I'm not bad at it, but I didn't intend to be around long enough to get to use that pool hall.

When we got back home, we could smell cookies baking. Aunt Mattie was spreading the hot ones out on the kitchen table, and we each took one.

"How bad was the damage to Mr. Fowler's car?" she asked.

"He'll have to replace a fender." Gramps got out the milk and poured us each a glass. "Have another cookie, boy."

Leroy was watching us with saliva gathering in the

corners of his mouth. When Aunt Mattie wasn't looking, Gramps slipped him a cookie which he swallowed whole.

"How did you know we saw the accident?" I asked as she put another pan into the oven.

Her lips flattened into a straight line. "Because Dad's always there when anything happens. I saw Mr. Fowler go past and heard the noise his car was making, like a fender rubbing on a tire. I knew Dad must have seen it. What's that dog doing in here?"

"Guess he thought he was invited," Gramps said. "Why don't you pick up a bag of dog food next time you're in town? Cheaper than feeding him cookies, I'd think."

"I have no intention of feeding him cookies . . . or anything else. He's not our dog, nor our responsibility, Dad."

"He likes Danny. And let's face it, somebody's gone off and left him. If he had a home, he'd go to it, wouldn't he? Wouldn't be hanging around here where the pickings are so lean. Wasn't there a bone left out of that roast the other night?"

"There's enough meat left on it for soup," Aunt Mattie protested, but Gramps was already poking around in the refrigerator.

"Not enough there to flavor the water," he pronounced. "Here, boy, you take this out on the grass and chew on it."

Leroy thumped his tail and politely carried the bone outside when I opened the screen.

Aunt Mattie scowled, but she didn't stop him.

"Every boy ought to have a dog," Gramps said.

"Not as big as that one."

"He and Danny are getting along fine. Be good company for each other, won't you, Danny?"

"Sure," I agreed. "He's a neat dog."

"It will be better when Danny meets some of the other children," Aunt Mattie said. "That little girl at the Hopes' is the only one on our side of the lake right now. I wish your father had brought you a little sooner, and I'd have tried to take you around to meet the rest of the youngsters. I don't have time, now. I have this bazaar to organize at the church, and my assistant is down with a fractured hip so I'll have to do her job as well. But I'm sure once school is open, you'll make lots of friends."

I didn't care whether I did or not. I wondered, if I wrote and told Dad how lonely I was, and bored and unhappy and depressed, if he'd send for me.

And then I knew I couldn't do that. He'd be ashamed of me for being such a baby.

I guess I felt like a baby, there for a while. After supper Gramps and I dried the dishes (and that was something I never had to do when we lived in hotels, either!) and then I went outside again and down to the lake.

This time Aunt Mattie didn't keep yelling at me every little while so I didn't have to pretend not to hear her. I suspected Gramps told her that eleven was old enough to be trusted to go down to the edge of a lake without getting into trouble. Boy, was I glad Gramps was there and I wasn't living with just Aunt Mattie.

I found out Leroy knew a few basic commands: sit and stay and fetch. He liked "fetch" the best, and I threw a stick for him. The first time I accidentally threw it into the lake, I thought he'd forget it, but he didn't. He swam out and brought it back and shook water all over me.

I sort of wanted to walk down the beach, but that Mr. Fowler was out in front of his place doing something with a small boat, and I didn't feel like talking to anybody. Finally he went inside, but it was nearly dark by then. I might as well wait for the next day, I thought, when I'd be able to see something if I investigated the Bernard house.

And then I saw them again. Lights. Far down the shore, quite a bit beyond the big cedar tree that marked the Bernard place. This time the prowlers weren't being quite so careless with the flashlights, because I only caught an occasional glimpse even though I stood there watching for about ten minutes. Just about the time I thought I'd imagined it, or the lights had gone away, I'd see them again.

"Hey!" I said to Leroy. "Maybe that Minden Curse *has* rubbed off onto me. If I had a flashlight of my own, I'd go down there right now and see what's going on. But we'll go tomorrow, you and me. Maybe they're robbers and they're looking for a place to stash the loot, and we'll find it and collect the reward. How about that?"

I didn't really believe that. I just wanted to think that something interesting was happening in Indian Lake, and that I'd get involved in it.

For a while I forgot about thinking up excuses for my dad to send for me and imagined getting my picture in the papers when I went up before the mayor to collect my reward.

When I mentioned the lights to Gramps, though, he wasn't offhand about them. He went and called the sheriff. That made me feel sort of foolish, because I couldn't even tell them for sure where the lights had been, just somewhere beyond the old cedar.

"It was only a couple of flashlights," I said. "I don't know that anybody was doing anything they weren't supposed to do."

"Well, after last night it might pay to have Ben check it out," Gramps decided. "There's no reason for anyone to be down at the end of the road with lights, not that I can think of." He looked at me and chuckled. "I do believe you got it, Danny."

I started to say, "You mean the Minden Curse?" but I saw Aunt Mattie's face, her mouth set in that straight line I was coming to know meant she didn't like whatever was taking place, so I didn't say anything. I'd just wait and see.

2

As soon as Aunt Mattie left to work on the preparations for the church bazaar the next morning, I whistled to Leroy.

"Let's go for a walk, boy," I told him.

Gramps didn't ask where I was going, or what I was going to do, or tell me when to come back. I was beginning to like Gramps.

I headed along the lake, past the empty houses, toward the place that had been broken into. Leroy trotted along ahead of me, pausing once in a while to make sure I was still coming. A couple of times he waded out in the water and stuck his nose and eyes under it to look at something.

We went past three houses that were all closed up, with shutters nailed over the windows, and then we came to a smaller place, no more than a cottage. It didn't have shutters, and there was a pair of rubber boots on the porch, and a sports car with a crumpled-up fender parked beside it.

Ahead of me, Leroy had picked up something off the beach. He stopped and was licking at it, and he looked at me and wagged his tail.

It was a dead fish. It hadn't started to smell too much yet. I didn't know if a dog ought to eat a whole fish or not, or if the bones were dangerous.

"Maybe you better leave that alone," I suggested.

Leroy wagged his tail.

"Maybe I better throw it out where you can't get it," I said.

I picked the fish up by the tail and heaved it as far as I could, out into the water. And two things happened that I didn't expect.

The fish floated, and Leroy went after it.

A minute later he was back, looking very proud of himself; he held the fish in his mouth and shook water all over me.

"Look, I think fishbones are dangerous. They get stuck in your throat," I said. "Give it to me, Leroy."

He didn't want to give it up, though. He thought it was a game, and he went galloping across the beach and up to the brown cottage. I went after him, yelling, "Here, Leroy!" but he didn't listen. He went right in the open front door.

Pretty soon after that I heard someone yell, and Leroy came back out the door, almost knocking me off the steps. He didn't have the fish.

Oh, boy.

Jerry Fowler came to the door. He was wearing the same jeans and tennis shoes, but no shirt. He was carrying the fish by the tail, and he looked as if it had rotted some in the past few minutes.

"Your dog left this," he said. And then he looked at me more closely. "Do I know you? Oh, you're Mr. Minden's grandson, aren't you?"

"Danny Minden," I said. "I'm sorry, Mr. Fowler, I tried to get the fish away from him because I didn't think he ought to eat it, but he swam out and got it."

"Then if it's all the same to you, I'll put it in my garbage can," he said. I told him that was all right with me, and he dropped the fish in and put the lid down tight. By this time Leroy was a quarter of a mile up the beach, chasing a bird.

"I hope he didn't do any damage," I said.

Jerry Fowler sucked in his cheeks. "He dropped the fish in the clean laundry. I'm afraid my wife won't like that."

"I'm sorry. Is there anything I can do . . . ?"

"No. I'll run it through the washer again before she gets back from town."

"I'll try to keep him away from here," I said. "He isn't really my dog, you see, but somebody went away and left him, Gramps says. So he's staying at our house."

Mr. Fowler looked as if he thought it would be

better if Leroy did stay right there, but he didn't say anything nasty. I thought that was nice of him.

I went past some more boarded-up houses. There must be a lot of people here in the summer. I wondered what they all did to entertain themselves.

A short distance up the beach I saw a kid, dressed about like me in jeans and a T-shirt, only he was barefoot. He turned when Leroy bounded up to him and made flapping motions, then cried out, "Get out of here! Go away!"

It wasn't a he, it was a she, I decided. Maybe that Hope kid they'd talked about.

Leroy took off after something, and the girl yelled at him, but Leroy didn't pay any attention. Then I saw that he was chasing a big black and white cat, and not until it went up a tree did he return to the beach with his tongue hanging out.

The girl was about my age, and the way her hair was cut you couldn't tell what she was. Only her voice was feminine.

"Is that your dog?" she demanded when I got a little closer.

"Sort of."

"What's that supposed to mean? Is he or isn't he? He chased Marcella."

"He didn't catch her," I pointed out. "I don't think he'd hurt her, anyway. He just wanted to play."

"Is he your dog?" she asked again.

"He's a stray. My grandpa's been feeding him." I was sure getting off to a good start with all the neighbors, thanks to Leroy. I supposed I'd better introduce myself. "I'm Danny Minden. I'm staying with my Aunt Mattie."

Judging by her appraising look, she wasn't too impressed with red hair and freckles. She had dark hair and greenish eyes, but I didn't think she was pretty, either.

"I'm C.B. Hope," she said finally, after I'd about decided she wasn't going to tell me. "I live up there."

She waved a hand toward the biggest of the houses I'd passed; it was all natural wood and stone and had its own dock.

"C.B. What kind of a name is that for a girl?" I wanted to know.

"It's my initials. They stand for Clarissa Beatrix," she said coldly, daring me to comment.

"Does everybody call you C.B.?"

"I refuse to answer to anything else," she stated. "So if they don't, I just don't answer."

I shrugged. I guess if my name was Clarissa Beatrix, I'd use my initials, too. I looked up in the tree where her cat was peering through the leaves, watching Leroy.

"Does your cat know how to get down from there?"

"We'll have to get the ladder and get her down.

Since your dog put her up there, you can carry the ladder," she said.

I got a feeling this girl was going to be too bossy to get very friendly with. But it was true Leroy had chased her cat, so I followed her up to the garage and brought back the ladder. Marcella only scratched me once while I was getting her down. When C.B. turned her loose, she shot for the house, with Leroy flying along behind her. He was graceful when he ran, actually, and he would have been nice to watch if C.B. hadn't been yelling at him to leave her cat alone.

Marcella made it under the porch, though, and Leroy gave up and started back toward us. All of a sudden he stopped and poked his nose into the grass. It was like lawn, but it wasn't mowed so it was pretty long; I guess all these summer people figured they were getting out in the wilds, they didn't need to cut their grass. Anyway, Leroy was excited about something; he jerked back and started to bark.

C.B. got there before I did, and I heard her yell. "Hey, cut that out, you rotten beast!"

For a minute I thought it was Leroy she was mad at again, and then she swooped down in the grass and came up with a snake in one hand and was pulling a big toad out of its mouth with the other hand.

"That's Icky, my pet toad!" She gave the snake a toss off into the grass and examined the toad. I just looked at her. Maybe Dad was right, I didn't know anything about other kids. I never thought girls picked up snakes and toads. "He's hurt," she said and showed me the toad.

The toad had been swallowed, one leg of him, right up to the hip, or whatever that part is on a toad. Anyway, the one leg was all brown colored, and he held it out straight instead of bent like the other one. And when C.B. touched it, you could tell it hurt.

"He was swallowed long enough for the snake's digestive juices to work on him," I said. "Looks like his leg's been dipped in acid or something. Maybe it would help to wash him off."

So we took him down to the lake and washed Icky off. He didn't like it, but C.B. said that was probably because his leg was hurt. Leroy wanted to see what we were doing, but when I said "No!" real sharply, he stopped trying to smell the toad.

The bad leg still dangled, like maybe it was broken.

"Do you think he'll be all right?" C.B. asked anxiously.

"I don't know. I guess you'll have to leave him where he can rest and see if it gets better."

We finally decided that under the porch was the safest place. He hopped once and sat there, a sad-looking toad.

"He's lived around here for two years," C.B. said. "He's a good toad. We put out sugar water for him sometimes, and he doesn't care if I pick him up. Until his leg was hurt, he didn't."

"Marcella's under there, too. Will she bother him?"

"She won't hurt him. She's probably gone by now, anyway. She just wanted to get away from your stupid dog."

"Leroy isn't stupid. Dogs just naturally chase cats." I whistled at Leroy, who was smelling around as if he'd like to investigate under the porch if he could get under there. "Let's go, boy."

C.B. looked at me. "There's nothing much interesting down that way."

There wasn't anything much interesting in any direction, so far as I knew. But I was curious about the house that had been broken into and the reappearance of the lights last night in a different spot.

"Where's the Bernard house? Is it that yellow one I can see through the trees?"

"They're gone," C.B. said. "They left a week ago."

"I know. But somebody tried to break in there night before last. I just thought I'd look around."

She made up her mind fast. "I'll show you," she offered, and so we all went along the edge of the lake, the girl and Leroy and me.

We didn't have any trouble figuring out where the house had been broken into, because the heavy wooden shutters had been pried off one window and the glass broken. Somebody had nailed a board across the opening, but it didn't keep us from looking in. It wouldn't keep anyone from getting in, either.

We debated a few minutes and decided it wouldn't matter if we went inside and looked around. After all, the burglars, or whatever they were, had already been in there. Probably the police had, too, because there was no sign they'd opened up the doors and gone in that way.

"We're not going to steal anything," C.B. said, "so the Bernards won't care if we just look."

She was pretty good at climbing in windows. She went in first, and I scrambled after her. Leroy stood on his hind legs and watched us, barking.

"Shut up," I told him, and he sort of grinned at me, his tongue hanging out. He sure was a tall dog when he stood up.

It was disappointing when we got inside, though. It was only an ordinary summer house, nothing fancy. The electricity was turned off, so we couldn't see too well, what with shutters over all the windows. It only had one little bedroom, and a bathroom with rusty stains in the tub, and the kitchen and living room.

"Doesn't look like they left any clues," I said. "Unless the police already collected whatever it was."

"If I was going to look for something to steal," C.B. said thoughtfully, "this is one of the last places on the lake I'd break into. The Bernards just furnished it with junk, and they don't leave their TV here or anything like that." She looked around the kitchen. Some of the cupboard doors were open, as if somebody'd been checking them out. There wasn't much inside but a few cans of vegetables and some Spam. "Hey. That's funny."

"What is?"

"The dog food." She picked up a can that was part of a stack at one end of the counter. "The Bernards don't have a dog."

"I've heard of people eating dog food because meat is too expensive," I said.

She made a face. "The Bernards aren't *that* poor. Maybe they had company who brought a dog with them, and they didn't bother to carry its food away again."

We didn't see anything else interesting at all. So we climbed back through the window, with Leroy licking my face all the way, and started back to the beach.

"I want to go on down that way," I said gesturing.

"There's nothing down there but more empty cottages," she said.

"OK. So I'll look at empty cottages. There were more lights last night, I saw them. Gramps called the sheriff, and he came out along the road but didn't see anything."

She brushed back a falling lock of dark hair. "When was that?"

"Just after dark I saw the lights. I guess maybe nine-thirty when Sheriff Newton checked it out.

Why? Did you see the lights too?"

She shook her head. "No. I heard the sheriff's car go by, though. He wasn't out there more than ten minutes or so. But after he'd gone back—I was upstairs reading and I saw the lights on top of his car, so I knew who it was—another car came out. I heard it, but I didn't see it. I thought it was funny their lights were out." She considered the implications of that, now, working her face into a scowl.

"Do you think it could have been somebody who didn't have any business down there and the sheriff didn't catch them at anything, but they sneaked out as soon as he'd gone? It's a dead end road, anyone who went down there would have to come back past here. What do you think they were doing?"

"You've lived here longer than I have. What is there to do?" I asked.

She made a face. "Not much of anything. Still, it wouldn't hurt to go take a look, would it?"

I agreed that it wouldn't, and we started on down around the edge of the lake. She waded in the water, watching her feet as she splashed.

"You going to go to school in Indian Lake?" C.B. asked.

"Yeah. For this year." I *hoped* that would be all.

"Me, too. We're not going back to our winter house this year." She didn't sound any happier about it than I did.

"Don't you know any of the kids that go here?"

She shrugged. "A few. Mostly, though, I played with the summer kids, the ones that live out here along the lake. The summer people and the year-round people don't mingle all that much. We're different social strata, I guess. Or is it stratas?"

"Strata is already plural, I think. The singular is stratum. Which level is higher, the summer people or the year-round ones?"

"I don't know. I guess each one thinks *they* are. I go to a neat school at home," she said. "We get to ride horses and play tennis and everything. We have an Olympic-size pool. They don't have *anything* in Indian Lake School. Besides, I know I'll hate it, going to a new place."

"Me, too. I never went to a school before," I said.

She stopped and stared at me. "Never? How come?"

So I told her how my dad travels all over taking pictures and writing stories about them, and how I got assignments from this teacher friend of Dad's and kept up the work that way, without having to actually go to a school.

She thought that sounded pretty good, except that there were no horses to ride or tennis or swimming pool. But we were in agreement about one thing, we didn't want to go to school in Indian Lake.

"They have this statue of an Indian chief standing

in the front hall," she said, "and there aren't even any Indians in the whole town. I think it's dumb."

I couldn't have agreed more. We were the same age, but she was a grade behind me. We wouldn't even have each other in our class, so we'd each know somebody.

Leroy was having a great time, running up and down the beach and bringing me sticks to throw for him. When my arm got tired, I told him, "No more," and he finally stopped pestering me.

I stopped and looked ahead, then back down the curving shoreline to a couple of birch trees I knew marked our property line. "I'm trying to figure out where the lights were, the second ones I saw. I think they might have been right up there, about where that old dock is falling apart."

C.B. wasn't pretty, but she had an interesting face when she was intrigued, and right now that's what she was. "You think it was the same people, both nights?"

"Unless there are two batches of weirdos running around at night with flashlights. And everybody says there's nothing for anyone to be doing out here at night. So what *were* they doing?"

She hunched her shoulders. "What do you think?"

"Maybe they're robbers looking for a safe place to stash their loot or to hole up until the cops stop looking for them or something."

The minute I said it I wished I hadn't. Maybe other kids didn't make up stuff like that, maybe she'd think I was a fool.

But she didn't laugh. She considered it quite seriously, and her head began to nod. "Could be. Or maybe they hid something a long time ago, last spring, and then the people who lived around here came for the summer and they couldn't get it back, whatever it was. So they had to wait until the houses were empty."

"If that was the case, why would they be looking at different houses? Wouldn't they know which one they hid the stuff in?"

She swatted a mosquito and looked at the bloody smear it left on her hand, then wiped it on her jeans. "Maybe one of the gang hid it, but something happened to him. And the others are going by what he said on his deathbed. If they were robbers, he could have been shot, and he couldn't tell them exactly which cottage he hid it in. It would have to be valuable, wouldn't it? A lot of money or jewels or something like that?" Her green eyes were practically shooting sparks of excitement. And I'd been afraid she'd ridicule my imagination!

"Let's go see," I said.

The last two cottages on our side of the lake were both small and dilapidated. That means they were all but falling down, compared to our house and the

Hopes'. They were shuttered the way Aunt Mattie had described, all closed up for the winter.

There'd been somebody at both of them, though, and we didn't think it had been very long ago. The ground was sandy and didn't hold prints well, but it was clear someone had driven into one driveway recently, and there was a cigarette butt.

"It rained two or three days ago," C.B. observed, "and that would have made it come apart. So it's been dropped since then."

We didn't find anything else, though. It was disappointing, although I guessed if there had been anything shady going on, the guys would have been smart enough not to leave much in the way of clues.

Still, the day wasn't a total loss. There was still the possibility that there was a mystery here, even if it wasn't as exciting as bank robbers or jewel thieves. I looked over at C.B. as we started toward home.

"You're not the way I thought girls would be," I observed.

The scowl worked its way over her face again. "What's that supposed to mean?"

"Nothing bad. Maybe my dad was right. He said I needed to get acquainted with kids my own age, and you're the first girl I've ever been around for more than a few minutes. I thought girls just played with dolls and stuff like that."

She made a snorting noise. "That was when I was

little. But I played with trucks, too. And rode horses and skated and did all the things boys do, if I felt like it." She splashed along the edge of the lake, and the water lured me into it, too. She tipped her head to look at me. "No kidding, didn't you ever do anything with other kids?"

"When I was little, before my mother died. But since then I've traveled with my dad, all over the country. He takes pictures and writes articles for *On the Spot* Magazine. You ever hear of it?"

"Sure." C.B. looked quite respectful. "My dad reads it all the time. So how come you had to come here, then? Did he get tired of dragging you around with him?"

I considered that. "I don't think so. He said he liked having me with him, and we always had a lot of fun together. But this assignment he's got in Ireland is going to take quite a while, and he didn't think it was the right place for me. Besides, I think what really happened is that Aunt Mattie finally got to him. She kept writing him these letters telling him I should be in a more stable atmosphere, in school with other kids."

I told her about it, how I'd argued with him until I was practically blue in the face. Just remembering gave me a sick feeling in my stomach all over again.

"I don't care about knowing a bunch of dumb kids," I'd said. "I want to go where you go."

"Maybe that's part of the problem, son," Dad had told me. "You don't want to know any kids, and that isn't normal. After your mother died I wanted to keep what was left of our family together, and it was selfish of me, considering the way I never stay put for more than a few months at a time. I've deprived you of a normal childhood."

"Boy, you never thought that up, Aunt Mattie said it," I yelled. "I don't feel deprived, so why all the fuss? How come everyone gets to put in their opinion but me?"

My dad is usually a great guy, but that day he wasn't bending an inch. "You need to be able to relate to your peers. And you can't. You don't know the first thing about how normal kids live."

"What are peers?" I wanted to know.

"Kids your own age."

"Look, what difference does it make if I know any kids or not? Pretty soon we'll all be grown-ups, and then we'll all be alike, right? Same age, no problems."

"Wrong. You'll be the same age, but you will never have experienced the things all the rest of them have. Never known what it was like to go to school . . ."

"I still don't see what's so important about it," I told C.B. "I was learning my lessons, getting good grades."

She shot me a look through her eyelashes. "Are you scared of going to school?"

I almost stumbled and fell in the water, and I pretended I'd stubbed my toe on a rock. "Heck, no! Why would I be afraid?"

She shrugged and jammed her hands into the pockets of her jeans. "I don't know. *I* am, I think. Well, maybe not exactly *afraid*, but nervous. I mean, I've spent every summer of my life here at Indian Lake, except for one year when my mother was sick and we stayed in town. And the only kids I ever played with were summer kids, like me. I don't think the Indian Lake kids like outsiders."

"You can't be an outsider if you've spent every summer of your life here," I protested, but I felt sort of hollow inside, because I had an inkling of what she meant. "If you don't fit in after all these years, where does that leave me?"

"If you're really good at something it might help." She looked hopeful.

"I get pretty good grades. At least I did doing things at home with Dad coaching. But I'm not much good at anything else, like playing ball. I guess that's what's impressive, isn't it? Being an athlete? I'm a fair swimmer."

"They don't have a pool here," C.B. said flatly. So I wouldn't impress anybody *that* way.

Leroy was running up and down the beach while we walked, and all of a sudden he started barking like crazy. I was going to yell at him to shut up, but then I saw what he was barking at.

There was this little kid, still in diapers he was so little, and he was walking out on the Hopes' dock.

There wasn't anybody in sight watching him, and we were still quite a ways off. C.B. yelled and started to run, and the little kid turned and looked at us, not paying attention to where he was going.

He fell right off the end of the dock into deep water.

3

C.B. had a head start on me, but I caught up with her right away. Jogging is one of Dad's things, because it's an exercise he can do no matter where we are, and I always jogged with him.

I looked at her face, and I could tell the kid meant something to her. I mean, anybody would try to save a little kid from drowning, but this one was special to her. There wasn't any way we could get there fast enough, I thought, and then I heard Leroy still barking like crazy. I yelled at him. "Fetch, Leroy! Fetch the baby!"

I don't know if he even heard me, he was making so much noise himself, but he ran right out on that dock and jumped into the water. I heard C.B. making distressed noises as I passed her.

Some people came out onto the porch of C.B.'s

house. I didn't have time to look at them, but one of them started to scream. "Toddy! Where's Toddy?"

I hit the dock with a thud that jarred me all the way up to my head, and I kept on running right out to the end. Luckily it wasn't a very long dock, but maybe it was already too late, even though we'd run as fast as we could.

Leroy was out of sight, but when I got to the end, there was his wet head, and he had a bit of cloth in his mouth . . . the diaper that was the only thing the little kid had on. Leroy swam toward me, and I laid down flat and got hold of the diaper, hoping to gosh it wouldn't slide off before I could grab the kid himself.

I fished him out, and he made noises, so I knew he wasn't drowned. He was choking and gasping and his blond hair was plastered to his head. C.B. came running out onto the dock, with the other people behind her. They were all yelling, and the two women were crying. One of them grabbed the baby out of my arms, and everybody was pretty relieved when he began to cry, too.

Leroy was still swimming around the end of the dock, and I got him to follow me toward shore. One of the women—I found out she was Mrs. Hope—came after me.

"Thank you. We'd never have reached him in time," she said. She wasn't hysterical like the baby's mother, but there were tears in her eyes.

"It was Leroy that saved him," I told her.

"But you called to him to fetch the baby," she said. "I heard you."

So they made quite a fuss. C.B. told me his name was Toddy and he was her sister's little boy, and only that morning their father had warned her to keep closer track of the kid because he was fascinated by the water.

I called to Leroy, and we went on down the beach. I guess he was as glad as I was to get away from all those excited females. Leroy shook himself all over me, so I was dampish when I went in the house.

Gramps was sitting there carving his birdcage. He looked at me over the tops of his glasses.

"Didn't you bring a bathing suit, son?" he asked.

Aunt Mattie was packing decorations of some kind into a box to take to the church. She looked over at me and then at Leroy, who was staring through the screen door. I'd thought he'd better stay outside until he dried off. "For pity's sake, what happened to you?"

"He fell in the lake, obviously," Gramps said. "Or else he decided to go swimming and it was too long a walk back for his swim suit."

"C.B.'s nephew fell off the dock," I said, "and Leroy went after him when I yelled fetch, and then I fished him out, and he got me all wet. And then Leroy shook all over me."

So of course they had to hear all the details. "So you just happened along at the right time to save him," Gramps said, sounding pleased.

"Well, it was Leroy got to him first. I couldn't run fast enough. And if Leroy hadn't held him up, I don't know if I could have brought him up quick enough or not," I said.

Gramps chuckled. "I think they both got it, Mattie. Danny and the dog. They both got the Minden Curse."

"I don't see how it can be a curse if it makes it possible for you to save somebody's life," I said.

Aunt Mattie made disapproving noises—of Gramps's fool ideas, not of me saving the baby—and picked up her box under one arm. "Well, see that that dog doesn't come in here while he's wet. I'm going to be busy at the church until late afternoon. You two can start supper; I left a list of instructions on the front of the refrigerator. I'll see you then."

As soon as the car drove away, Leroy began to whine.

"He had anything to eat yet today?" Gramps asked.

"I gave him a pancake. He swallowed it in two gulps."

"One pancake isn't much for a critter that size." Gramps opened the door and let Leroy into the kitchen. "Should have reminded Mattie again to get some dog food for him. Can't get rid of a dog that saves lives, now can we?"

So we fed him bread and milk, and then we found out we were supposed to have milk for supper and we'd used it all up. Gramps sighed and put aside his birdcage.

"Well, son, looks like we've got to go to town. You might as well come with me and help carry things, and we'll get the dog food, too."

So we went to town, and that was how we happened to be there when the bank was robbed.

After we'd walked all the way to town, Gramps found out he didn't have enough money for the stuff we wanted, nor his checkbook, either, so we went over to the bank. Gramps told Leroy to "stay" on the sidewalk outside when we went in.

I wouldn't have thought a town the size of Indian Lake would have a bank. It was the littlest one I ever saw; it had those grille things for two tellers, only I never saw more than one of them open at once. There was a raised brick platform thing in the middle of the lobby, and it had an old wood-burning stove on it. Gramps said they actually used it in the winter, although they had electric heat, too.

The lady in the teller's cage said, "Hello, Mr. Minden," and Gramps said, "I forgot my checkbook and I need another ten dollars, Sandra," so she made him sign something and gave him the ten dollars.

He didn't even have it in his pocket yet when we heard somebody say, "All right, everybody stand right where you are."

We all turned around and looked at these two guys who'd just come in. One of them closed the front door and pulled down the shade. I could read the word CLOSED, backwards, written on the shade.

They were just ordinary looking guys in jeans and T-shirts and big sunglasses that hid their eyes. Only one of them was carrying a gun, and it was pointed right at Gramps.

There wasn't anybody in the place except us and Sandra, the teller, and Mr. Zazorian, the bank manager. He was sitting at a desk behind a little half-wall sort of thing, and he started to get up, with his mouth open.

"Sit down," the guy with the blue glasses said, and Mr. Zazorian sank back onto his chair.

The one with the brown glasses (the other one had the gun) came toward us and said, "Put all the money in this sack."

Sandra looked at her boss, and he nodded his head. He'd closed his mouth by this time, but he opened it to say, "Give it to him."

The guy with the brown glasses passed a brown paper bag under the bars to the teller, and she opened a drawer and put money into the sack and gave it back. Gramps and I just stood there watching.

The robber looked in the sack. "Is that all you've got?" he asked. Then he saw Gramps still holding his ten dollar bill, and he reached out and took it and dropped it in the sack. "There isn't enough here to make it worthwhile," he told his partner.

"That's all there is," Sandra said. "I've cashed a lot of checks today."

"There's got to be more in the vault," the one with the gun said. He waved it at Mr. Zazorian. "Open the vault."

"This is a small bank," Mr. Zazorian said. "We don't keep much cash on hand."

"Open the vault anyway," the guy said.

So Mr. Zazorian went into the little back room, and the guy with the gun stood where he could watch all of us, and we just stood there until a few more bundles of bills went into the paper sack.

The guy with the blue glasses took out a red handkerchief and wiped off his face. It wasn't all that hot, but he sure was sweating. He stuck the handkerchief back in his hip pocket.

I was trying to see something about the robbers that would help identify them later, but there wasn't anything unusual. No birthmarks or tattoos or scars. They both had medium brown hair that needed cutting.

The one with the brown glasses closed up the paper sack. "Now," he said, "all of you go in the back room and stay there for ten minutes. Don't come out unless you want to get shot."

So we all went into that little back room, and there

was hardly room for four people. The robber closed the door, which was made of iron bars like a gate, locked it with the key that was in the lock, and threw the key in a wastebasket.

They went out the front door, leaving the CLOSED sign on the shade.

Mr. Zazorian said a few swear words, and then apologized to Sandra. "Everybody will think we're still out to lunch; they may not rescue us for hours."

Sandra moved up to the ironwork door. "Maybe I can get my arm out and reach the telephone on your desk," she said.

But she couldn't reach between the bars; she stuck at the elbow.

"Let me try," I said. My arm was skinnier than hers. I couldn't reach the telephone, either, but Gramps had an idea.

"The cord comes out from the wall. See if you can get hold of the cord there on the floor, Danny, and pull the phone off the desk."

So that's what I did. It made a racket when it hit the floor, and there was a crack in it, but I could still hear a dial tone. So they told me the number to dial for the sheriff, and I held the receiver so Mr. Zazorian could talk to him through the bars. A few minutes later the sheriff came to let us out.

His name was Ben Newton. He wore a tan uniform with a badge on it, and he was mad.

"What's this town coming to? Breaking and entering night before last and now a bank robbery! How much they get, George?" he asked Mr. Zazorian.

"All there was. Maybe six thousand," Mr. Zazorian said.

"And my ten dollars," Gramps said. "Dadburned robbers, they took my ten dollars, and I still can't pay for my groceries!"

"Ben will get it back. Won't you, Ben?" Mr. Zazorian said hopefully.

The sheriff scowled. "What did they look like?"

We told him, all talking at once. Ben Newton didn't look any happier. "That could be anybody. All they have to do is take off their sunglasses, and they look like everybody else in town! Jeans and T-shirts!"

By this time he'd got the key out of the wastebasket and let us out. We looked up and down the main street, and there were people around, but none of them was wearing big sunglasses and carrying a brown paper bag.

Ben Newton yelled to an old man sitting across the street. "Hey, Pete, you see anybody come out of the bank carrying a sack?"

The old man shook his head. "Didn't pay no attention, Ben. Bunch of young fellers in town, whole busload of 'em. Going to a work camp or something. Bus had an accident 'bout twenty minutes ago, ran into Harley's pickup, and they ain't got the road cleared yet. So the boys off the bus came to town to get something cold to drink, I reckon. Anyways, most of 'em are either in the Red Barn or Winnie's place."

"State patrol at the scene of the accident?" the sheriff said, looking as if he felt a little better. "If the road's blocked, the robbers didn't go that way. I'll get on the radio and make sure, and then set up a roadblock out the other side of town."

"So the robbers can't get away," Mr. Zazorian said hopefully. "Can they?"

"All we got to do is find out which of the thirty or so young men in town did it," Gramps said. "I bet you every one of 'em is wearing jeans and a T-shirt."

"The robbers are carrying a brown paper bag," Sandra reminded us.

"Pretty easy to stash that somewhere if they've found out they can't get out of town with it," Ben Newton said. "Stash it anyplace and come back and get it later."

"Well, let's spread out and see if we can find them," Gramps said.

"I'll take Leroy with me," I offered. And then when we got out on the sidewalk I spotted something. "Hey look! The guy with the blue glasses dropped his handkerchief!"

Nobody else seemed as excited as I was about it.

"Plain old farmer's bandana," the sheriff said. "Can't be over a hundred of 'em in town."

I picked it up and held it under Leroy's nose. "Smell that, boy? Can you find the guy that smells like that?"

The sheriff snorted. "That's no bloodhound you got there, boy. Come on, let's check out every place on Main Street and see if we can find our men."

Nobody said I was to do anything in particular. I let Leroy sniff some more. "Come on, boy. Let's see if we can find them," I told him, and he wagged his tail and looked as if he wanted to help me.

We didn't seem to get anywhere very fast, though. There were plenty of guys in town, like the old man had said. College-age guys. We could rule out the ones that didn't have brown hair, but that still left about seventy-five percent of them. And practically all of them were wearing old jeans and T-shirts.

Leroy didn't pay any attention to any of them. I wished now I'd looked closer at their shoes: had the robbers worn sneakers, or leather ones? I couldn't remember. Most of the fellows I saw milling around with hamburgers and soft drinks wore either sneakers or combat boots; a couple wore sandals. I was pretty sure the robbers hadn't worn sandals; I thought I would have noticed that.

The sheriff and Gramps and Mr. Zazorian were going along the street checking out every business place. Sandra went back to the bank. She said she was nervous about being there all alone after what had happened, but Mr. Zazorian told her there was nothing left to steal, so why be nervous?

"Well, shoot," I told Leroy. "Mostly what we saw was brown hair and those big blue and brown sunglasses. If they took off the glasses, we aren't going to know them when we see them."

Leroy wagged his tail. He was resting in the shade while I thought. When I held out the handkerchief again, he smelled it; I could tell he wanted to be helpful, but he didn't know what I had in mind.

"Fetch," I said. That had worked when the baby fell in the water. "Find something that smells like this, and fetch it, OK?"

He sniffed obediently, and then got up and trotted into an alley between the bank and the hardware store. It didn't seem a likely place for the robbers to have gone; they certainly couldn't have parked a getaway car back there. The alley was a dead end because there was a gate at the far end of it. Beyond the gate I could see some garbage cans.

"I don't think you got the idea yet," I told Leroy, but he trotted right along, back to the gate. He smelled all around the gate, and tried to poke his head through it, but he was too big.

"What do you want? Those guys didn't go over the gate, there's nothing to get a toehold on. And if they'd opened it, I doubt if they'd have stopped to close it again."

Leroy whined and pawed around. Then he looked at me and waited.

I didn't believe it, but I didn't have anything else to do. I unfastened the latch and let the gate open so we could go through.

Leroy made straight for the garbage cans. He knocked one of them over and the lid fell off, and orange peelings and coffee grounds and other junk spilled out. He poked around in it with his nose, picked up a bit of something and ate it.

I watched him in disgust. "Just because you didn't get anything to eat today but a pancake and bread and milk! We've got serious business to tend to, and you're knocking over garbage cans."

He didn't pay any attention to me, but knocked over the other garbage can. This time the lid rolled off and clanged into the back of the building, and a fat man came to the door and yelled at us.

"Hey, what do you think you're doing? You clean up that mess, and get your dog out of there!"

Leroy ignored the man, too, and poked around. I felt sort of embarrassed. First the fish and then saving the baby and now dumping garbage in the alley. I just couldn't tell which way Leroy was going to go.

"You hear me?" the man demanded, taking a few steps toward us.

And then I forgot about him, because I saw a familiar brown paper bag festooned with a used typewriter ribbon and some wilted lettuce leaves.

Leroy had found the money.

4

The man who owned the garbage cans was pretty irritated until I opened the bag and showed him. "The robbers must have hid it there, thinking they'd come back and get it when the roads were open so they could get out of town. It looks like it's all here, even Gramps's ten dollar bill. It had a red mark in one corner. See?"

Then the man didn't even insist that I pick up the garbage. He went with us to find the sheriff. Leroy pranced along beside us, looking very pleased with himself. I was pleased with him, myself.

So was everybody else. Mr. Zazorian counted out the money and said as far as he could tell it was all there. He gave Gramps the ten dollar bill with the red mark on it. The sheriff wanted the bag and its contents to check for fingerprints. "If those guys got a record, we'll find them."

Mr. Zazorian said if the sheriff took all the money how was he going to operate his bank? And the sheriff said if they didn't check for fingerprints, how was he going to catch the robbers?

Gramps said, "Come on, boy, let's get our groceries and go home." By now it was way past lunchtime, and we were all hungry, so Gramps bought us each a hamburger to last until we got home, and two for Leroy. I carried the dog food, and Gramps carried the milk and the rest of the stuff. Leroy just trotted along having a good time with a bit of onion clinging to his whiskers.

After we'd walked all the way from town in the hot sun, we no more than got into the house when Aunt Mattie drove up. She looked upset.

"Are you both all right? Aggie heard you'd both been involved in a bank robbery!"

"We weren't exactly involved," Gramps said, putting the milk into the refrigerator. "We were sort of bystanders, I'd say. We didn't get shot or anything like that."

"Leroy found the money," I told her. "In a garbage can."

"I don't think you realize what it's like," she said to her father. "Always having people come up and ask if I know what's happened to you this time. I can't believe the things you get mixed up in, and it's getting worse."

"I told you, the boy's got the Minden Curse, same as I have. I think even that goldanged dog has it."

"Aggie said they had a gun!"

"That they did. Aggie say if they found the robbers, yet?"

"No. I mean, no, she didn't say. What are you doing?"

"Fixing a lunch. We didn't have enough money for more than a hamburger apiece in town, and I couldn't get any more from the bank. The sheriff wanted to check it all for fingerprints before he gave it back. You like peanut butter and honey, Danny?"

Aunt Mattie decided she was too busy to fool around with us. She stopped when she was almost out the door, though. "Oh, that reminds me. Aggie gave me the key to the Miller place. She's authorized to rent it out, and there's some fellow wants to look at it this afternoon. She's going to be helping me at the church, though, so when he comes you take him over there, will you?"

And then she was gone, and we could eat in peace. As Gramps said, "She's a good woman, Mattie is, but she carries on some. Here, let's use this for a dog dish. Fill up, Leroy."

Leroy nibbled a little of the dog food, but you could tell what he really wanted was part of our sandwiches. Finally we made him one of his own, and he liked that just fine.

There was a telephone call in the middle of the

afternoon. Gramps handed it to me. "It's your dad. Must be calling from New York." He went out on the porch so I could talk in private. A real diplomat, Gramps was.

"Hi, Danny. How things going?" Dad said. He sounded like he was in the next room, so I figured he hadn't got to Ireland yet.

"Oh, pretty good," I said. "Where are you?"

"Kennedy Airport. My plane leaves in twenty minutes, so I figured I'd check on you. I really hated to leave you, son, but I think it's for the best. I know Indian Lake is a dull place, though, after the places you've been with me."

"Oh, it hasn't been as dull as I expected," I said.

I thought he was surprised. "Oh? You meeting people already, are you?"

I thought about the baby falling off the dock and the fish on the Fowlers' clean laundry and the burglarized house and the bank robbery. Then I remembered that his plane left in twenty minutes and decided maybe I'd better write it all to him in a letter.

"We've got a dog," I said. "He's part Irish wolf-hound. His name's Leroy."

"That's great." He sounded relieved. "Well, tell Aunt Mattie I said hello. I'll write to you when I get to Ireland. I hope you like it there."

I didn't any more than hang up when the phone rang again. This time it was for Gramps. The sheriff had rounded up a couple of suspects and wanted us to come in and identify them. Sandra said she was too scared to notice anything, and Mr. Zazorian said he couldn't tell without their colored glasses.

"Well, we can't both come at once," Gramps said. "We got to take some fellow over to look at the Miller place this afternoon. Mattie just left us the key. And we've already had one long hot walk today. I'm an old man, Ben. How about a ride in the police car?"

Ben must have said yes, because Gramps was smiling when he hung up. "Tell you what, Danny. I'll give you the key, and you show the fellow the Miller place, and I'll go identify the robbers."

"But I don't even know where the Miller place is," I protested. Besides, I thought it would be more fun to identify the robbers.

"Oh, you can't miss it. It's the last place at the end of the road, halfway around the lake. And there's a sign, says Miller's Hideaway. There's the key on the table. All you have to do is let them in to look around. If they decide they want it, they can go talk to Aggie over at the church and pay her the rent money."

"I don't remember where the church is, either." It didn't seem quite fair. I saw the robbers just as much as he did, and I don't wear glasses.

"Only three churches in town, and you can see 'em all from Main Street," Gramps said. He was looking out the window to see if the police car was coming yet. "Community Church is the white one with the tallest spire. Can't miss it."

I was disappointed, and I guess he saw that.

"Don't worry. If I can't say for sure these are the right ones, I'll have Ben take you in to look at 'em, too. Ah, here's Ben! No siren, but he's moving right along. See you later, son," he said, and away he went.

I didn't dare go away from the house, so I found something to read and sat on the porch in the shade.

Half an hour later Gramps hadn't come back, and a beat-up old station wagon pulled in the driveway. A guy got out and came across the grass.

He wasn't very big, and he was skinny, and he seemed nervous. He was smoking a cigarette, and he dropped it in the grass and stepped on it. Then he looked all around as if somebody might catch him at it.

"Uh, this the Minden place?" he asked.

He had an adam's apple that made him look as if he had a yo-yo in his throat, the way it went up and down.

"Yes," I said. "Are you the man who wants to look at the Miller place?"

I couldn't tell if he was nodding his head or if that was just a nervous mannerism. "Yeah. Yeah," he said. "Name's Royce. Royce."

"I'm supposed to show it to you," I told him. "I haven't been there, but it's the last house at the end of the road, and there's a sign."

"Yeah. Yeah. I know. I mean, I drove out there and saw it. From the outside, I mean."

"I'll get the key," I said, and a few minutes later we were on our way.

As Gramps said, we didn't have any trouble finding the place. Just beyond the driveway with the sign, the road ended in a jumble of blackberry vines.

When we got to the house, I wondered why he'd picked this one to want to rent. It needed paint, and it was practically falling down. It made the Bernard cottage seem positively elegant by comparison.

Nobody'd cut the grass for a long time. There was a rusted bicycle lying in the weeds by the back door. And the view of the lake wasn't even very good, the cottage was so far back in the trees. The mosquito population was high, too. I swatted one on my arm when we got out of the car.

"Kind of isolated," I said. "All the summer people have gone home for the winter, so you wouldn't have any neighbors until spring."

"That's all right. My wife—my wife, she's been sick. Needs the peace and quiet, don't want any visitors. Besides, we won't be here more than a couple of weeks. Just need a rest. A rest," he said.

I figured what the heck, it was no skin off my teeth if he wanted to spend a couple of weeks in this ratty little shack. I unlocked the door, and we went inside.

I didn't know if they had cockroaches in the country, but if they did, I was willing to bet this place had some. Mr. Royce turned on the faucet, and a trickle of rusty-looking water ran into the sink.

"Water works. I guess the electricity would have to be turned on?"

I flicked a switch and nothing happened. "Yes, it looks that way."

We moved through the place. I didn't touch much of anything. It was that kind of place. Mr. Royce opened a bedroom door and looked at the sagging bed, then peered into the saddest looking bathroom I ever saw.

"Maybe some of the other places are for rent," I suggested. "There are nicer places, closer to town."

He stared through the trees toward the lake. It was a rocky stretch of beach so there wouldn't even be good swimming, but maybe they didn't want to swim.

"I could ask my aunt," I said. "She knows everybody."

Mr. Royce sighed. His adam's apple was bobbing up and down as if he was trying to swallow a ping-pong ball. "No. This will do. I guess I'll have to write a check for that lady, what's her name, Aggie Kirk."

I thought he was crazy, but it was his money. If he wanted to spend his vacation, or whatever it was, in this dump, that was his business.

When we drove into our yard, the sheriff's car was

just leaving. Mr. Royce stared at it.

"Is that the police?"

"Yes. The sheriff's just bringing my grandfather home. He didn't do anything," I explained quickly, in case he should get the wrong idea. "We were in the bank when it was robbed today, and he had to go identify the robbers."

"The bank was robbed? In this little place?" He stopped the car and lit a cigarette. I never saw anybody so nervous. He knocked the hot ashes into his lap and had to brush like mad to get them off. I wondered if it wasn't him that needed the rest, instead of his wife. "Well, thanks for showing me the house."

I was glad to get out of his car. Mr. Royce smelled as if he didn't take a bath often enough. I wondered if he was used to living in a place like the Millers' cottage.

Leroy got up and came to meet me and lick my hand. He had a very gentle tongue for such a big dog. We both went inside.

Gramps was getting a drink of iced tea out of the refrigerator. "Find the place all right, did you?"

"Sure. He wants to rent it. He's not very particular."

Gramps offered me some of the tea, but I decided I'd rather have plain water. "Guess that place is getting in bad shape. Nobody lived in it this year at all; old man had a stroke and they stayed with their daughter. Funny time of year to be renting a cottage, when the good weather is about gone and everybody's moving back to the cities."

"Yeah," I agreed, and wondered what I was going to do until suppertime. "Did the sheriff catch the right people, the ones that robbed the bank?"

"That he did. He put the garbage back into the cans behind Yolinski's place and then found him a spot where he could watch them. Sure enough, once the road was cleared and the bus loaded up and went on, two fellows came back and looked in the garbage can. They denied everything at first, but when he found a pair of blue and a pair of brown sunglasses in their car, he figured he had them. I knew the minute I looked at 'em they were the ones."

"It took you quite a while," I said, and then wondered if that sounded rude.

"Well, I had my picture taken. You know, for the weekly paper. Mattie thinks I get my picture in the paper too often, but they wanted all of us in it. Sandra and Mr. Zazorian and me. Would have included you, too, if you'd been there."

I didn't know what kind of answer I was supposed to make to that, so I figured I'd better not say anything. I'd rather have been having my picture taken than been showing Mr. Royce that crummy old cottage.

We fixed the stuff we'd been told to put in the oven for supper. I could see Gramps knew quite a lot about cooking.

"Oh, Mattie's always busy with something for the church. Or once in a while she substitutes for a teacher that's out sick. So I got used to doing for myself. Good idea for a man to know how to cook; keeps you from starving sometimes."

We were all ready to eat when C.B. came to the door with a tall man she introduced to me as her father. He'd come over to thank me for saving Toddy's life. I told him it was Leroy as much as me, so he shook my hand and patted Leroy on the head and told Aunt Mattie she'd ought to be proud of me.

The whole thing was pretty embarrassing. I was glad when they went home and we could sit down at the table.

"I was talking to Paul Engstrom's mother at the church today," Aunt Mattie said. "He's in your grade in school, Danny. I suggested it would be nice if you boys got to know each other, and she said she'd send him out to meet you."

I mumbled something and hoped he'd forget about it. I really didn't care about getting acquainted with some kid who was going to find out I didn't play baseball (you don't get a chance when you move around so much) and who, if he was in my grade, was probably so big he'd make me look like a midget.

I found some good books to read and took them into my room. When Aunt Mattie wasn't looking, I l t Leroy in with me. Both Aunt Mattie and Gramps slept upstairs, and they had given me the guest room on the ground floor. It was just a room, old-fashioned after the hotel rooms I'd slept in, but it had a good bed, hard the way I like it.

It was a good thing it was a double bed, because that night Leroy decided he'd sleep with me. I didn't invite him to, but I woke up in the night dreaming I was being squashed by a steamroller, and it was Leroy. After I convinced him that he could only have half the bed, I went back to sleep.

I guess it must have been after midnight when I woke up again because Leroy was pushing me out of bed. I tried shoving him over, but he wouldn't go, so finally I got up to go around the other side and get in there.

I don't know why I looked out the window. It was open, with a screen to keep out the mosquitoes, and a nice breeze blew off the lake. Everything was really quiet; they had TV in Indian Lake, but the stations both went off after the eleven o'clock news, so there wasn't anybody sitting up watching the late movie.

There was a light on out across the water. I hadn't seen one there the night before, so I stood looking at it a minute, trying to think where it would be. And then I figured out it had to be the Miller cottage, halfway around the lake.

I almost laughed at the thought of anybody trying to burglarize *that* place. No junk man would have offered ten dollars for the entire thing.

By that time I was more or less awake, and I was thirsty. So I went out and got a drink, and got one for Leroy, too. When I went back in the bedroom, the lights were still there, only moving.

Exactly like the flashlights two nights before at the Bernard place. I stood there a minute, watching. At least two people were carrying flashlights and moving around. The more I thought about it, the funnier it seemed. I mean, it was an old wreck of a place, and anybody could tell from the outside that there wouldn't be anything valuable in it. Yet at the end of the road, that way, it wasn't a house a casual traveler would just happen to come upon. Especially at midnight.

Leroy went to the door and asked to go out. I pushed open the screen, and then I decided I wasn't very sleepy and I'd go outside, too.

One time when Dad and I were in Florida (he was taking pictures of fishermen catching swordfish), we'd get up at night when it was hot, or early in the morning, and rush out in our pajamas and jump in the water. I didn't think the people around Indian Lake would necessarily approve of that, though, and I didn't want Aunt Mattie to be embarrassed by anything I did, so I got dressed before I went out.

Leroy showed up the minute I hit the beach; he greeted me with a big sloppy lick on the hand, and then tore off ahead of me.

It was a nice night. No moon, but lots of stars; I was surprised, there were so many more than I was used to. I finally figured out it must be that more of them were visible because there wasn't any city nearby to light up the sky.

It wasn't exactly warm; I'd grabbed a long-sleeved shirt and it felt good. I didn't have shoes on, though, and when I accidentally waded in the water, I found it felt warmer than it had during the day, so I kept on walking in it. A kid could go for a long time without washing his feet if he walked along the lake every day, because the sand really scours them.

All the houses were dark when I went by. But every once in a while I caught a glimpse of the moving lights over across the lake. I didn't exactly decide to go see what was going on, I just kept on walking, with Leroy running ahead of me, until the next thing I knew I was almost there.

Leroy had disappeared in the shadows under the trees, and I was about to whistle for him when I heard the commotion.

Something banged and rattled like a bucket dropped down the stairs, and then a man's voice started cursing and I heard Leroy bark, just once, and another crash. Oh, boy.

I hurried toward the old Miller cottage, and a man said, "That thing was as big as a moose! What was it?"

The second voice was one I recognized. "I think it was a dog," Mr. Royce said, but he didn't sound sure of it.

There was some more profanity. "I never saw a dog that big in my life. It was the size of a pony."

I stood there in the shadows, wondering if I ought to let them know I was there. After all, it was my dog; maybe I ought to acknowledge him. On the other hand, if they were mad maybe I'd be better off not to. I couldn't do anything about whatever he'd made them drop.

I didn't even know where Leroy was. He'd disappeared into the woods. They had the station wagon parked near the door to the cottage, and they were hauling stuff inside. It looked as if they were just about finished. One of the men was picking up some canned goods from the steps, using the flashlight to look under the porch.

Behind me, I heard Leroy, and I turned in relief and started moving away. "Come on, stupid, stay away from them," I whispered, and grabbed him by the collar.

Just the new tenants moving in, I thought. Nothing very exciting about that, although it was a peculiar time of day to do it. Midnight, by flashlight. They didn't even have the electricity turned on yet, or surely they'd have had the lights on so they could see better.

I went back along the lake, wading in the water, and hoped Leroy wouldn't cause any more trouble for a while.

5

Aunt Mattie didn't seem too happy about it when the man from the newspaper showed up the next morning to take pictures.

"It's bad enough my father gets his picture in there nearly every week," she said, "and now you want to take Danny's picture, too."

He was a young man with a broad grin and hair even redder than mine. "What's wrong with having your picture in the paper? I was thinking of taking yours, too. You're running the bazaar at the Community Church, aren't you? That's newsworthy, too."

"Me?" Aunt Mattie said. "Oh, you don't mean now, do you? My hair isn't fixed."

"Well, why don't I get your picture at the church? Say Saturday afternoon, when you have the decorations set up, and then we'll run it in next week's paper."

Aunt Mattie considered that, then nodded, half-pleased, half-embarrassed. "Well, I guess that would be all right. I have to run, there's so much to do. I'll be back at lunchtime, Dad."

The reporter winked at me when she went out the door. "Bless the ladies, sometimes you have to turn their attention to something else when they don't want you to do your duty. And my duty is to cover the news, including pictures of the boy and the dog who recovered the money after the bank robbery. How did you know where to look for it, Danny? Did you figure they'd ditched it?"

"I didn't really figure much of anything," I admitted. "I had the handkerchief one of them dropped, and I thought maybe Leroy could smell it and then find the guy who smelled the same way. The sheriff said he wasn't a bloodhound so he probably couldn't do it. But he just went right along to where the paper bag was, in the garbage can, so I guess he must have smelled the trail. Maybe he has a little bit of blood-hound in him."

Gramps chuckled. "I'd say Leroy has a wide assortment of dog varieties in him. He going to be in the picture, too?"

"We'll say DOG DETECTIVE, or something like that. Come on, Danny, you and Leroy come out on the porch and we'll get five or six shots, be sure we've got a good one."

He was still taking pictures, talking a mile a minute to get me to smile, when C.B. came along. She stood there watching. Leroy sat beside me on the steps as if he had his picture taken every day.

"Are you taking his picture because he saved my little nephew?" C.B. asked when the reporter was about finished.

So then he had to hear all about that, and we spent half an hour going over to the Hope house, where he took a lot more pictures, of Toddy and Leroy, and Toddy and me, and Toddy and his mother, and some more of Leroy and me out on the dock. He said, "Can you get your dog to dive in the water again, so I can get a shot of him swimming?" So I threw a stick off the end of the dock and told Leroy to fetch.

"Gosh," the reporter said, "I wonder if I can get the boss to let me have a whole page about the wonder dog and his boy."

"Aunt Mattie'd have a fit," I said uneasily. "Maybe you better not overdo it."

He didn't make any promises, but he seemed very pleased with himself when he took off for town.

"You come over for something special?" I asked C.B.

She shrugged. She was wearing a striped knit shirt and cut-off jeans, today, and ragged sneakers. I thought girls wore dresses some of the time, but this one didn't seem to. "I thought maybe you'd like to go pick apples."

"Pick apples! Hey, that sounds like a fantastic thing to do!"

She gave me a withering glance. "You don't have to be sarcastic. If you don't want to go, all you have to do is say so."

"Why would I want to pick apples?" I asked. I had never picked apples, but it sounded like work.

"Because my mom makes real good apple pies, if someone else will pick the apples. And there are some getting ripe on the old Shaver place."

"I'm going to learn the name of every house in the entire county. Where's the Shaver place? Don't they object if you pick their apples?"

"It's only the orchard left, now, just a little way beyond Miller's cottage. The house fell down years ago, and anybody who wants the apples enough to walk in and pick them can have them."

"I thought the Miller place was at the end of the road."

"Some berry bushes have grown over the road because nobody uses it anymore. But we can get to the orchard along the lake. Mom says she'll give your aunt a whole pie if you'll help me pick the apples."

If there's anything I like, it's apple pie. Not the kind you usually get in a restaurant, but the kind Aunt Mattie makes at Thanksgiving, with lots of butter and cinnamon in it.

"What the heck, there's nothing else to do," I said.

So we stopped up at her house to get a couple of plastic buckets, and C.B. said maybe it would take us a while to get them full so she made us a couple of sandwiches to take along.

Jerry Fowler was out doing something to his car when we passed his place. A pretty girl in blue shorts was sitting on the porch polishing a pair of shoes. I figured she was his wife and thought maybe I'd better not stop, in case she'd heard about the dead fish in her laundry basket.

But Mr. Fowler saw us and waved and came down on the beach. "Hi. Going after berries?"

"Apples," C.B. said. "The berries are all dried up."

"Oh." He looked at me. "I hear you're a hero."

"I don't know why they have to put anything in the newspaper around here," I said. "Everybody already knows all about it before the paper even comes out."

"Oh, we like to read about it anyway," he said. "I understand you're both going to school here this year."

"Yeah," we both said, without enthusiasm.

"Well, don't sound so overjoyed! We have a nice school. I'll bet you'll like it."

"I'll bet *I* won't," I said.

He laughed and said I had a very pessimistic attitude for a young hero and went back to work on his car.

"Why do grown-ups always think you ought to

enjoy school?" I asked.

"He's a teacher," C.B. said. "Didn't you know? He teaches sixth, seventh, and eighth grade math. His wife, Jean, teaches first grade."

"Oh, wow! Thanks a lot for warning me."

"How did I know what you were going to say to him?"

"I hope people aren't going to keep referring to me as a hero," I said. I picked up a rock and threw it into the water, and all of a sudden Leroy came galloping out of the trees and dived in after it. "Look at that stupid dog. I didn't tell him to fetch."

He went down three times and came up with a rock the last time. When he brought it back to me, he stood there panting, after he shook water all over us, waiting for me to throw it again. "Nuts to you," I said and dropped it in the sand. Leroy looked disappointed for a few minutes, then took off ahead of us.

"What's wrong with being a hero?" C.B. wanted to know.

"It's embarrassing."

"I don't see why it should be. Hey, look, there's somebody sitting out in front of the Miller place!"

"Yeah, they moved in last night. At midnight, imagine!"

"Somebody's living there?"

"A Mr. Royce and his wife. And there was another guy helping him last night. They're renting it for a few weeks. His wife's been sick or something and wants to rest."

"If I wanted to rest, I would've picked a better place than that. It's the crummiest cottage on the whole lake," C.B. said.

"I think it's cheap. He doesn't look as if he has much money," I told her. "Leroy scared them. They thought he was a wild animal I guess, and they dropped the stuff they were carrying."

"Were you down there watching them at midnight?" She turned to look at me with those big green eyes.

"We went for a walk and just happened to be there. I wasn't exactly watching them. Besides, all they were doing was carrying stuff from the car into the house."

There were two people on the beach, sitting on a log. One of them got up and went toward the cottage. The one left was Mr. Royce. He didn't seem happy to see us. Especially not Leroy, who ran up and shook water all over him and then rolled in the sand.

"Hi!" C.B. said, and I waved a hand. Now he'd know. Leroy was my dog.

He didn't say anything about Leroy, though. He sniffed, and his adam's apple bobbed up and down. "What are you kids doing way down here? I thought this was a private beach."

"There isn't any such thing as a private beach," C.B. informed him. "At least, nobody's ever objected to anyone walking around the edge of the lake."

"You're a long way from home," he said, looking sour. He took out a cigarette, lit it, and left it dangling from the corner of his mouth.

"Not so very. We're going to pick apples." C.B. waved her hand. "Over there, there's an old orchard. Maybe your wife would like to pick some, too. They don't belong to anyone anymore."

"My wife? No, no, my wife don't feel good enough to pick apples."

"Oh. I'm sorry if she's sick." C.B. smiled at him, and we kept on walking. "Did you get the impression he didn't like us walking past his cottage?"

"Who knows? Where are these marvelous apples?"

We had to walk back from the beach eventually, and there was the old orchard. I'd been expecting red apples, but these were green. It was too early for the red ones, C.B. said. These were transparents, and they made good pies and good sauce.

The best ones all seemed to be up high, so we climbed into the trees. C.B. was enjoying herself, but if this was what Dad meant about getting to know how other kids lived, then I didn't see what was so important about it.

After a while, though, when I had my bucket filled, I sort of mellowed. I mean, it wasn't really unpleasant up there in the tree, looking out over the lake, smelling the apples.

"I'm hungry," I said to C.B. "Let's take a break and eat those sandwiches. My pail's full, anyway; how about yours?"

"All we'll need for pies," she agreed, and we climbed down and went over to where we'd left our lunch sack.

The sack was there, all right. But the lunch wasn't. I stared into the bag in disbelief. "You made two sandwiches apiece, didn't you?"

"And some cookies," C.B. confirmed. She glanced around us. There wasn't much of anything to see except apple trees, and the lake on one side and the tall grass on the other. There were some berry bushes and some trees away from the lake.

"If that confounded Leroy ate our lunch," I said, beginning to be annoyed.

"I haven't seen Leroy for a long time, though," C.B. observed. "He started chasing a rabbit or something out through the woods. Maybe it was a bear. My mother met a bear once, not too far from here. She was picking blackberries and heard this noise, and there was a bear on the other side of the bush, picking berries, too."

I didn't know whether to believe her or not. The woods looked thick enough so they *could* have had bears in them, though. It made me feel peculiar, but I wasn't going to start running for home. Not and have her think I was a big coward. Afterward I got to thinking that was stupid; better to be a coward than to be eaten by a bear. But I was really hungry, and all there was left was an empty bag, and it was a long walk home. Of course there were the apples, but I'd already eaten one of those and didn't want any more.

"Leroy!" I yelled, but no familiar pony-sized dog came bounding through the grass. A minute later C.B. pounced on something with a cry of triumph.

"Here's one of the sandwich bags! And look, there are teeth marks in it. It must have been Leroy."

Disgusted, we headed for home.

We hadn't gone very far when I had to switch hands, carrying the bucket. C.B. did, too, but she didn't say anything about its being too heavy. I began to think that half a pail apiece would make plenty of pies, but with a girl carrying the same amount as I was, I couldn't quite say so.

This time when we went past the cottage Mr. Royce wasn't outside, but we heard voices through the open door. I couldn't quite make out the words, but Mr. Royce sounded angry about something.

"Hey, I have an idea," I said. "If Mrs. Royce isn't well enough to pick apples, maybe she'd like some just to eat. We've got plenty."

"OK, let's ask them," C.B. agreed, and we went up onto the rickety porch and knocked.

"Darned fool, I told you to watch . . ." Mr. Royce

was saying, and then stopped when he heard us. He came to the door, and he looked even less pleased to see us than he had the last time. "Whadda you want?"

"We thought maybe you'd like some apples. We've got a lot," I said and held up the pail. If he took enough of them, the rest would be easier to carry.

"We don't like apples," he said. Rude, he was. Not even a "no, thanks," just *we don't like apples*.

It was embarrassing. I mean, if I talked to anybody like that, my dad would jump all over me. Mr. Royce obviously wasn't very well brought up.

He just stood there looking at us, filling the doorway so we couldn't see much of anything in the room behind him. Not that the room was much, I'd seen that before, but I was kind of curious about his wife, the one that was so sick, but he still yelled at her. I didn't see her, though.

C.B. was smiling at him just as if he'd been polite. "My mother's going to make them into pies. Do you like pie? We could bring one back for you."

Mr. Royce's adam's apple was fascinating to watch. I wondered if he didn't have trouble swallowing past it when he ate. It bobbed up and down, and his scowl looked as if it had been chiseled into his face.

"No, we don't need any pie either. Beat it."

And he shut the door right in our faces.

"Well," C.B. said. She finally got the message. "I guess he doesn't like us."

"So who cares? Come on, let's go home and get something to eat." I bit into an apple, it was easier to eat one than carry it. My arm was falling out, and I switched the pail to the other hand. "I wonder where my dumb dog went? I'll bet he knows he shouldn't have eaten our lunch."

We plodded along in the sand, and pretty soon we met Leroy. He was wet, as if he'd been swimming, and he galloped up with that fool grin on his face, friendly as ever.

"You stinker," I said. "We didn't get anything to eat."

"All four sandwiches and half a dozen oatmeal cookies," C.B. added. "You're a greedy pig, Leroy."

He just looked at us and wagged his tail, then poked his nose into a bucket of apples. He decided he didn't want one of those. No wonder, after eating our entire lunch.

We left the apples with Mrs. Hope, and C.B. asked if I wanted to come back and go swimming after our lunches had time to digest so we wouldn't get cramps. I thought it sounded like more fun than picking apples, so I said OK.

Gramps was sitting on the porch overlooking the lake when I got home, carving on the birdcage. The bars were all done, and he was beginning to work on the lump of wood in the middle of it, but it didn't look like a bird yet. He put it down and looked at me.

"I gave up on you for lunch. There's chocolate pudding in the ice box and cold roast for sandwiches."

"The ice box?" I echoed.

He made a snorting sound. "Ah, they used to be ice boxes. Habit is a long-lasting thing, I guess. I suppose that dog wants to be fed, too."

"He shouldn't need much," I said. "C.B. made four sandwiches, and there were cookies, too, and he ate them all while we were picking apples."

Gramps seemed to find that amusing. Maybe it would be funnier to me after my stomach was filled, I thought. While I ate, Gramps dumped dog food into the old pie tin on the floor, and Leroy ate every bit of it and then stood watching me until I gave him a crust.

"I know he's big, but he can't be completely hollow, can he?" I asked. Leroy thumped his tail, as if I'd said something complimentary about him.

"Your Aunt Mattie called," Gramps said, and something in his tone alerted me.

"Oh? What about?"

"She wants you to meet some kids before school starts, so she's bringing home Paul Engstrom for supper."

"Oh." I didn't even like the sound of the kid's name. Paul. The only Paul I ever knew was a radio announcer acquaintance of my dad's, and he was so stuck on himself it's a wonder he didn't wear his arm out, patting himself on the back. "Am I supposed to do something with him?"

Gramps chuckled. "Well, I suppose Mattie would be happy if you took to each other. Take him down to the lake if you want."

"That'll be a big thrill for him, I'm sure. There's a public beach for the town kids at the end of the lake, isn't there?"

"Yep. And a private one at the Lodge on beyond that. You have a point. I don't reckon he'd be thrilled by the lake. You could just talk to him. Get to know each other."

"What do you talk about to a kid you never saw before?" I wanted to know.

"Oh, you'll think of something. More'n likely he's heard about your exploits with the bank robbers and little Toddy. That'll give you an opening."

"The story hasn't been in the paper yet," I reminded him.

"Oh, he'll have heard it. Everybody just reads the details in the paper to see if they match up with what they already know. Who's that coming, Jerry Fowler?"

It was. Mr. Fowler stood outside the screened door, looking in at us until Gramps called, "Come on in, Jerry!"

I wondered if he changed out of those old jeans and the sweatshirt when he taught school. He ignored the chair Gramps swung around for him and looked at Leroy who was licking crumbs under my chair.

"Make yourself to home," Gramps said.

Jerry Fowler sighed. "I can't stay, thanks. I have to run into town and get some meat for supper. Look, Mr. Minden, I hate to come visiting with complaints, but I'm afraid Jean is pretty annoyed, and it's only fair to tell you."

We both stared at him.

"What have I done to annoy your wife?" Gramps asked. "She see me outside in my skivvies, getting in the pants Mattie left on the clothesline? Good woman, Mattie is, but when she gets busy with church affairs she sometimes forgets a man can't put on his pants while they're hanging on the line."

Mr. Fowler shook his head. "No, nothing like that. It's your dog."

"Leroy? What's he been up to?"

"I know he's a good dog. I mean, I heard about him rescuing the baby and finding the money that was stolen from the bank, and all that. And I'd hate to suggest you keep him tied up. But it's the second time he's been in our place, and Jean thinks I ought to mention it to you."

I looked at Leroy, who was watching me hopefully. I swallowed the last of my pudding before it strangled me.

"What's he done?" Gramps asked.

"The first time it was a fish. This time he stole the hot dogs Jean was defrosting for supper."

"He stole your fish, and then your hot dogs? Criminentally, dog, don't we feed you at home?" Gramps asked. Leroy just wagged his tail.

"He didn't steal a fish," I said "He found it on the beach, a dead one, and he took it into the Fowlers' cabin and dropped it on some clean laundry."

"Well, at least he tries to be fair," Gramps said. "Brings you something, then takes something. Ummm. Not funny, eh?"

"Not to Jean."

"How much you figure the hot dogs were worth?" Gramps said, reaching for his hip pocket.

"No, no, I don't want you to pay for them. I just thought maybe you could keep a closer eye on him, that's all. I'll try, too, not to leave the door open so he can get in. But we're used to having it open on nice days, and if I forget, well, my wife's easier to live with if she's not mad about something. You know."

"I know," Gramps agreed. "Well, we'll see what we can do, Jerry. And thanks for telling us."

After Mr. Fowler was gone, we stood looking at Leroy. He was totally unrepentant. In fact, he came and licked at my hand to see if I had any more to eat.

"I can't believe it. All in one day, all that food. And he had dog food earlier this morning. I gave it to him myself," I said.

"You did?" Gramps looked down at the pie pan, licked as clean as if it had just been washed. "Mattie gave him the leftover pancakes this morning, too, and I slipped him a sausage. Wonder if he's got worms. He ought to be round as a ball, eating all that, but I can still feel his ribs."

"Look, stupid," I told Leroy. "If you don't behave, we'll have to tie you up. No chasing cats or birds or swimming in the lake or having any fun. Understand? You only eat at home."

Leroy wagged his tail some more, and went out on the porch in the sunshine. I'd read for an hour or so, until it was time to swim with C.B., and I hoped the fool dog would stay out of trouble for a while.

6

Paul Engstrom was about the way I'd imagined him. Bigger than I was (he was twelve) and tanned as if he'd spent the whole summer outdoors and a mean look in his eye.

Not that he said anything mean, not at first. In fact he didn't say much of anything, just nodded when Aunt Mattie introduced us. I could tell he hadn't wanted to come to dinner any more than I had wanted him to come.

"Now, you boys just make friends," Aunt Mattie said cheerfully. "I'll get supper ready in a bit. Why don't you walk down by the lake; it's nice out there now, and I'll call you when it's time to eat."

In mutual disinterest, we walked down off the front porch toward the water. Away down the shore I could see C.B. sitting on the edge of their dock, dangling her feet in the water. She had Marcella on her lap.

I cleared my throat, trying to think of something to say. I already knew Paul was in the same grade I was; Aunt Mattie had said so. I also knew that as the host I was supposed to be the one to initiate the conversation. Initiate means to begin, but I didn't know how.

C.B. waved, and I waved back, feeling uncomfortable, though I wasn't sure why.

"Who's that?" Paul asked.

"C.B. Hope. She lives down there. She's going to school here this year, too."

"A girl?" He said it as if they didn't have much use for girls at Indian Lake School.

"She's not bad," I said. In fact, we'd had fun swimming that afternoon, off her dock.

"Neither are you, I guess," Paul said. He sounded sort of funny, and when I looked at him I read the hostility in his face. No kidding, he looked as if he really disliked me.

"What's that supposed to mean?" Host or not, my own antipathy was rising. Antipathy is one of those words that mean the same as hostility; this guy didn't like me, even though he'd never seen me before. So much for making friends with my peers, I thought sourly.

"I saw all those fancy photographs of you and your dog." He glanced at Leroy, who was diving for rocks in the shallow water. "A full page story they're going to have in the paper. Famous boy and dog heroes!"

There was no other word for it, Paul Engstrom was *sneering* at me.

"How'd you see the pictures?" For a minute curiosity won out over resentment. "He just took them this morning, and they aren't supposed to be in the paper until next week."

"My dad works on the paper. I was in there when they were looking at the pictures. A whole page!"

I shrugged. "Don't blame me for that. I don't want a full page of pictures in the paper. Aunt Mattie will be in a tizzy, too. She's already upset enough about what they call the Minden Curse, and if it touches me, too, she'll probably think it's even worse than when they take pictures of Gramps."

Curiosity got to him, too. "The Minden Curse? What's that?"

"That's what makes Gramps always be there when anything exciting happens. He says maybe Leroy and I have it, too, the way things have happened since I've been here."

"You mean the way your grandfather is always around when there's an accident or fire or a bank robbery?"

"Something like that."

"Sounds like a bunch of baloney to me." The antagonism was back.

"Yeah, me too. Still, funny things seem to happen."

I decided to make one try to do what Aunt Mattie wanted. "This will be a new experience for me, going to school. Do you like it at Indian Lake?"

He shrugged. "It's a school. Who likes to go to school? Arithmetic, ugh! And English is even worse. Writing essays and stuff. What's the sense of learning all that, spelling and verbs and stuff?"

"My dad is a photojournalist, and I guess he couldn't be one if he hadn't learned all that English stuff. I agree with you about the math, though. I'm not very good at it. My dad always helped me if I got stuck. I hope Gramps knows something about it."

"You mean there's something you *aren't* good at?"

"Lots of things," I said, "like playing ball. I never even tried that, so I don't suppose I'll be much good. Not at first, anyway."

I've heard about people's mouths dropping open, but this was the first time I'd ever actually seen it happen.

"You never tried playing ball? You mean baseball?"

"I mean any kind of ball. Baseball, basketball, football . . . I never played ball."

"The way your aunt talked, I thought you were perfect at everything," he said. He was looking at me as if he didn't believe what I'd said, and if it was a joke he was going to be mad about it. "A grade ahead for your age, good marks in everything. And then a hero, on top of all that! How come you don't like playing ball games?"

"I didn't say I didn't *like* ball games, I said I never played any. I never went to school before, so I never had a chance."

I had to explain about that, and I think it made him feel better that I wasn't perfect. Aunt Mattie meant well, but she sure wasn't getting me off to a good start if she made all the kids dislike me before they ever saw me.

He started telling me then how every kid in Indian Lake played ball, and how they had teams that played neighboring schools on Saturday afternoons. His favorite kind of ball was baseball, and he was the catcher, and he was a good hitter, too.

"We have a club," he said. "The Secret Club. You have to prove you aren't chicken in order to get into it. I've been asked to join. They don't invite just anybody."

I got the idea, all right. Full page of pictures and hero-story in the paper notwithstanding, I was going to have to prove myself when school started. It made me nervous, just thinking about it. What if all those peers my dad talked about decided they didn't want anything to do with me?

Aunt Mattie called us in to supper about that time, and while we ate, we didn't talk much. His mother came after him about seven, apologizing for being early, but I could see Paul was happy to leave. He hadn't decided to hate me, maybe, but he hadn't made up his mind to want me for a buddy, either. In fact, what little talking he did was about his friend Steve, who was the best pitcher in town, even counting the high school kids.

"Well, that was nice, wasn't it?" Aunt Mattie said happily when the Engstroms had gone.

"Yeah, sure," I agreed, but Gramps was watching me, and I could see he wasn't fooled that I'd made any points.

Aunt Mattie chattered on about how we'd better get my clothes in order, be sure I had plenty of everything for when school started, and get all the supplies I'd need like notebooks and stuff. It would have been easy to get depressed about the whole thing.

"Shoes," she said. "I notice you only have those sneakers. We'd better get you some regular shoes. Your father gave me the money for whatever you need."

"What's the matter with sneakers? They're what I always wear," I protested. "I've got a pair of old ones and a pair of good ones. I don't want any other kind."

So then I had to listen to how sneakers aren't good for your feet, and I showed her the supports inside, and Gramps winked at me like, *oh, you know women*, but I couldn't work up to being as amused as he was.

I got a book and took it in my room to read as soon as I could get away. I wondered if my mother would have gone on like that if she'd lived and been the one to raise me. I didn't think so. Dad said she was always a lot of fun and never a spoilsport about anything.

I was still reading when Aunt Mattie stuck her head in the door to say good night.

"Don't stay up too late, now," she said. "We'll go in tomorrow and see about the shoes and things."

It seemed a waste of money, because I knew I was going to wear sneakers no matter what we bought. I went out in the kitchen and fixed a sandwich and a glass of milk. Leroy lifted his head.

He looked hopefully at the sandwich. "You glutton, you've had enough for two dogs already today," I told him, but he still acted hungry. He even ate the dog food I put in the pie pan for him, and then waited for my last bite of sandwich.

He was a pretty smart dog. When only Gramps and I were there, he knew he could be in the kitchen or in my bedroom. When Aunt Mattie was home, he either played it safe by staying on the porch or being very quiet in a corner where she wouldn't notice him.

But at night he came along into my bedroom and jumped up on the foot of the bed. Just like he belonged there. I finished the book and got ready for bed, and after a short tussle we figured out who was going to have which side of the bed, and I went to sleep.

That is, I almost went to sleep. I was sort of beginning to dream about being in Ireland with my dad, taking pictures of those old houses built of little round stones, when Leroy started to whimper.

I guess it was a whimper. He raised his head and made this noise, and then he jumped off the bed and went to the window and made it again, only louder.

Then he really cried and scratched at the window and tried to stick his head out through the screen.

I sat up. "Hey, what's the matter with you?"

I could hear his tail wagging; it hit the side of the dresser with a thumping sound, and he pushed on the screen so I was afraid he'd push it right out.

"Cut it out, Leroy. Is there somebody out there?"

I crawled out of bed and tried to see out on the porch, but it was too dark to see anything. I held Leroy's muzzle so he'd be quiet and I listened, but I didn't hear anything.

When I let go of him, he stopped trying to get out. Funny, I thought. He'd acted like it was a friend out there, but outside of Gramps and C.B. and me I couldn't think who that would be. It was late enough so it wasn't likely to be C.B., and Gramps was asleep upstairs.

I got back into bed, and this time Leroy didn't keep me awake. When I opened my eyes again, the sun was shining.

C.B. came over before I'd finished eating my corn-flakes. Aunt Mattie invited her inside, and she stood by the door, swinging a bucket in each hand.

"Mom says she'll pay us to pick some more apples. She's going to sell pies at the church bazaar. For charity," C.B. said, to make it harder for me to refuse to go.

"Danny has to go into town and buy some shoes, but I suppose he could meet me there late this afternoon," Aunt Mattie said. "I'll go on over to the church; we have things just about ready, now. So you go ahead and pick the apples. Mrs. Hope makes marvelous apple pies; they'll bring a good price, and some people will come to the bazaar just to have a chance to get them."

I wasn't thrilled about picking more apples . . . especially not if we had to carry them all the way home . . . but there wasn't much of anything else to do.

"This time," I said, "I'll pack the lunch, and we'll put it in something Leroy can't get into."

He wagged his tail as if I'd said something nice about him. I found a Karo Syrup can, one of those with a handle and lid on top, and packed the sandwiches and cookies into it. Gramps told us that when he was a kid he used to carry his lunch in a Karo Syrup can when he went to school, and one time he got the wrong one. On a stormy day when he'd walked through snowdrifts up to his hips, a mile and a half to school, he got there and found out he had a can of syrup instead of his sandwiches.

"Got pretty hungry that day," he told us, laughing. "My friend gave me half a sandwich, but I was almost empty enough to drink the syrup before I got home. You kids have a good time today. You taking Leroy with you?"

"Haven't figured out any way to stop him going," I said. "I guess if we're going way down the beach, I'd better wear shoes. For the tough part when we go across the field."

I went out on the porch to get the sneakers I'd left drying there. That was one thing Aunt Mattie didn't seem to understand, that sneakers were something you could wear in the water if you needed to. You couldn't do that with regular shoes.

There was only one shoe on the porch.

I looked at Leroy. "Did you do something with my shoe? Come on, where is it?"

Gramps was getting settled in his rocker with the cage that had a wooden bird growing inside it. "Both of 'em were there when I let him in last night, unless you turned him out again after I went up to bed."

"No, I didn't. Then who took my shoe?"

I looked around, but I couldn't find the other one, so I had to wear my good ones. I was thinking about Leroy whining and trying to get out the window last night. Maybe someone—or something—had been taking my shoe right then. Next time I'd pay attention to him when he acted like that.

It wasn't a very exciting morning. We picked apples and had our lunch (Leroy ate part of it, but at least C.B. and I got our share) and then hauled the apples back to Mrs. Hope. When we passed the Miller place, it was all closed up tight and the old station wagon was gone.

"I guess his wife is feeling better today so they've gone somewhere," C.B. said.

I grunted. My arms were pulling out of their sockets with the weight of two pails of apples. "Just as well. Probably they'd tell us to stop walking past their place. They aren't very friendly."

We had to rest a few times, getting the apples back. Mrs. Hope said she'd appreciate some help peeling them, too, but I told her I had to go buy some shoes and I couldn't stay.

Leroy and I went on toward home. Mrs. Fowler was out on the beach, and when Leroy went bounding up, showering her with sand, she turned to face me. She was carrying a red sandal in one hand, and she was barefoot.

"Hi," I said, and then I noticed she wasn't looking very friendly.

"I don't suppose you've seen the mate to this?" She held up the sandal.

"No." It looked like a practically new shoe, not like the old sneaker I was missing.

Jean Fowler stared at Leroy, who was digging

furiously in the sand at the edge of the water. "I left them just outside the door, the way I usually do when I've waxed the kitchen. And when I went to get them, there was only one shoe there."

"I don't see how Leroy could have had anything to do with it," I said quickly. "He slept in the house with me last night, and he's been right with me all day. We've been picking apples since early this morning, and he was right there with us." I could see she wasn't buying that, because her scowl got deeper. "I left my shoes on the porch, too, and one of them is missing. Leroy heard something last night and fussed to get out, but I didn't see anything and I didn't turn him loose. It must be some wild animal or something."

"It's a fifteen dollar pair of sandals," Mrs. Fowler said.

I swallowed. "No kidding, you can ask Gramps if my shoe wasn't missing this morning. I'm going to town to buy some more this afternoon. And Leroy wasn't loose, honest he wasn't."

She sighed. "Well, if you find a red sandal, let me know."

"Yeah. Sure, I will," I assured her. I wondered if Leroy could have taken her shoe. I mean, he was there while we were picking apples, but naturally I didn't watch him every single minute. Still, if Leroy couldn't have swiped *my* sneaker, why wasn't it reasonable to think whoever took *it* also took Mrs. Fowler's sandal?

Gramps was ready to leave when I got home.

"Sheriff called. He's got a statement typed up for me to sign, and you, too. Figured we'd go ahead and get your shoes when we got that done," he said.

So we took off for town.

I told him about the second missing shoe.

"Maybe a porcupine or some other animal looking for salt," he said. "Sometimes shoes have salt on the inside, from where a person has perspired. And wild animals can't always find a good source of salt."

If it was a porcupine, I wished I'd seen it. I never saw one outside of a zoo.

We went into the sheriff's office, which was so little there was hardly room for the three of us; he had me read through a statement that said all I remembered about the bank robbery, and then I signed it. Gramps's statement was longer, and it looked as if they were going to chat awhile, so I went back outside where it was cooler.

And that's how I happened to be there when Mrs. Trentwood drove right into the fire hydrant, and I forgot how warm I was because the water sprayed all over me.

7

She was driving a big fancy car, pale blue inside and out. She was a lady about Aunt Mattie's age, I guess, and sort of plump, too, but that was all the similarity between them. Mrs. Trentwood had blonde hair that looked as if she just came from the beauty parlor, and she wore enough rings and necklaces and stuff to have been royalty. C.B. told me later everybody knew it was all real, mostly diamonds, she said. Mrs. Trentwood wore her jewelry even when she went walking on the beach, and the natives thought she was a bit odd but nice. She owned the Lodge on the opposite side of the lake from our place, and she spent part of every summer there. She owned other hotels, too, and she was very rich.

Of course, I didn't know all that when she drove into the fire hydrant. I knew it was an expensive car, naturally; any idiot could have told that.

I was leaning up against the front of the building, waiting for Gramps and wondering if I was going to have to wear regular shoes all winter instead of sneakers, when this car came along the street.

I noticed it because it was different from the other cars in Indian Lake. The ones parked along the street were dusty, instead of looking as if they'd just come out of the showroom, and they were older and less expensive models. Like station wagons and mini-buses and pickups, mostly.

Her car looked as if it should have a chauffeur driving it.

She was driving it herself, though, and I thought she was going to park in the space in front of the sheriff's office, although there was a fire hydrant on the corner and the curb was painted red so you weren't supposed to park there.

But she didn't park. She drove right up on the sidewalk and over the hydrant. It was an ordinary hydrant, painted bright yellow, and anybody could have seen it was there.

It made a horrible noise. Worse than when the man with the truck ran into Mr. Fowler's sports car. I could see the woman's face through the windshield, her mouth open in horror. She stopped, and then put the car in reverse and backed off, and the water squirted up in the air almost as high as the buildings.

It didn't take very long for about fifty people to show up, including Gramps and the sheriff. They all stood around and watched. I was all wet because I hadn't moved fast enough. Leroy was shaking himself dry.

"Bert," Sheriff Newton said to one of the men in the crowd, "go in my office and call Tom House, will you? Tell him there's a broken hydrant." He stepped closer to the pale blue car and peered inside. "Well, hello, Mrs. Trentwood. Have a little accident, did you?"

The water was showering all over her car, but the sheriff didn't seem to notice he was getting wet, too. The woman's mouth worked, but I didn't hear her say anything.

"You all right? You're not hurt, are you?"

She shook her head. "No. No, I'm not hurt. Oh, dear, I don't know how it happened . . . can you fix it?"

"Oh, sure, Tom House will come over and turn off the water and take care of it. I guess we'll have to file a report on it. Wait a minute until I get my pad and a pencil."

Mrs. Trentwood didn't get out of the car. She just sat there, and I could see she was shaking. After Ben Newton wrote down her statement—which wasn't much because she didn't know what happened, all of a sudden she'd just driven right over the hydrant—

and he asked would she come back the next day and sign the report after he got it typed up, Gramps went back inside to sign *his* statement.

The man came and turned off the water, and by that time everybody else was going on about his own business except for me and Leroy.

"I don't know if you ought to drive, Mrs. Trentwood," the sheriff said. "You're pretty shook up. Maybe somebody better drive you back to the Lodge when you're ready to go. You have some errands you wanted to take care of first?"

Her hand was resting on the edge of the open window, and for a minute I thought she was going to reach out and take hold of him. But then she shook her head and said, "No. No, I think I'll just go . . . I'm all right, Mr. Newton. I'll be careful."

I guess he decided she could do it, all right, because he went back into his office. I could hear the radio squawking in there, and then his voice answering it.

If he'd stayed outside and watched, I don't think he would have let Mrs. Trentwood drive home alone.

She backed up and bumped a motorcycle somebody had parked there. It fell over, but it didn't seem to be hurt much. And then she pulled ahead with a jerk and nearly ran over Leroy; he backed off and stared at her in astonishment. And after that she pulled ahead and made a U-turn in the middle of the main street, right under the sign that said NO U-TURN, and headed back in the direction she'd come from.

She must have come to town for something, but whatever it was, she hadn't done it. I wondered if she'd forgotten what it was.

Gramps came out shaking his head. "Well, at least she can afford to pay the damage. Fire hydrants are expensive," he said, and we went on down the street toward the shoe store.

Aunt Mattie met us there. Her lips were pressed tight together; and I knew why when the store clerk looked at Gramps and said, "What happened out there, Mr. Minden?"

I didn't mention that it was me who was the closest, who actually saw the accident happen. I knew Aunt Mattie hated to think another member of the family had the Curse.

I tried on shoes, and we bought a pair of brown leather ones. Then Gramps insisted on getting sneakers, too, since one of my old ones had disappeared. "He'll want those to muck around in," Gramps said, and I was grateful for that. At least I wouldn't be stuck with nothing but heavy shoes that had to be polished every week and kept out of the mud.

When we came out of the shoe store, I saw Mr. Royce. He was getting into his old beat-up car. I looked at the other person with him, because I was curious about his wife, who was sick yet was content to live in such a crummy cottage.

But it wasn't a woman with him, it was a man, the man who'd been helping him unload the night they moved into the Miller place. I wondered if the guy was staying with them, because it was an awfully small cottage for three people.

"As long as we're all in town, we might as well get the rest of the things Danny needs," Aunt Mattie was saying, and I turned away from Mr. Royce and his friend and followed her into the department store. Probably I just imagined it, I thought, that Mr. Royce didn't want me to notice him. Maybe I was getting a complex about people not liking me.

That weekend was the big bazaar. You'd think Aunt Mattie was running the whole thing single-handed, the amount of time she had to spend there. We fixed our own breakfast Saturday morning, and ate half of one of the pies Mrs. Hope had sent over. C.B. was right about one thing, her mom sure knew how to make apple pie.

Aunt Mattie drafted Gramps and me to run errands. There were people who'd ordered things even if they didn't intend to come to the church, and we got to deliver them. Half the women in town must have donated baked goods. The way I figured, each one made something, and then they all bought something someone else made, and the money went to the church building fund.

Anyway, I learned my way around town. Gramps drove the car, and I took in the baked goods and collected the money. At each place Gramps would tell me who lived there and what they did for a living and interesting particulars about them. I had to admit there were some interesting people in Indian Lake.

Like Mrs. Smithers, who was eighty-six and a peanut-butter-aholic. No kidding, she had a terrible craving for peanut butter, and she kept a jar under her bed in case she wanted some during the night. She seemed quite normal otherwise, and she bought a dozen peanut-butter cookies and a chocolate layer cake.

Another one was Bill Allenduff, a friend of Gramps's, who was a former archery champion. He had a big collection of bows and trophies, and he invited me to come back some day when I had time to hear all his stories. I promised I would.

And there was Paddy O'Hara, who was in a wheelchair. Paddy was old, too, and he had white hair and bright blue eyes and he laughed all the time. Paddy, Gramps said, had lost both legs when he was run over by a train. That sounded so gruesome I didn't even want to take his sugared doughnuts and apple pie into the house to him; but once I met him, it wasn't gruesome at all. He was a very jolly man who fixed watches to earn a living and made miniature ships for a hobby. He showed me a few ships and told me to come back for a whole afternoon and he'd tell me about all the other ones he'd built.

And then there were the kids. My peers, Dad called them. The ones I was supposed to get acquainted with because it would be good for me to know people my own age.

The trouble was, where the older people were perfectly friendly, the kids seemed to be suspicious. Everybody in town knew I'd never gone to school before, and for some reason this set me apart from all the rest of them. Some of them weren't hostile, the way Paul Engstrom had been, but I didn't meet any I thought were really friendly, either.

Only C.B. had treated me as an equal, and she was an outsider, too.

I had an uneasy hunch that making friends first with someone who wasn't a native, and was a girl on top of that, wouldn't make me any points with the guys at Indian Lake School.

The last place we delivered pies to was Indian Lake Lodge.

I'd seen it across the lake, a big log-cabin type of place where rich tourists stayed. It was past the season now, and usually they closed it up for the winter by the time school started, Gramps said. It was still open, though, with only a few guests. And Mrs. Trentwood was still there.

She owned the place, but she didn't run it; she had

a manager to do that. She just liked to stay in her own suite of rooms there. So I didn't expect to see her when I carried in the pies; but there she was, in the lobby talking to a couple who were checking out.

She took the pies and paid me for them. I thought she looked as if she'd been crying, but she had a lot of powder on so it was hard to be sure. She frowned a little bit.

"Do I know you?"

"I'm Danny Minden. I live across the lake," I explained. I thought maybe it would be unkind to remind her where she'd seen me, but she remembered by herself.

"You were there in front of the . . . yesterday," she said. "When I ran into that fire hydrant."

"Yes, ma'am."

"I was upset," she told me. "I'm usually a very careful driver, but I was so upset I couldn't think straight. I hope you don't believe I usually do things like that."

"No, ma'am," I said. I started edging toward the door.

"You had a dog. An enormous dog."

"Leroy. He's part Irish wolfhound."

"So huge. I like little dogs," she said, and her lower lip quivered.

"I like all kinds of dogs," I said. It was alarming to watch a grown woman's eyes fill with tears. I wondered if there was something I ought to say or do, but I couldn't think what. "Well, thanks for buying the pies."

"What?" She'd forgotten about the pies. "Oh, yes. Thank you for bringing them. Danny? Is that your name? Danny?"

To tell the truth, she made me uncomfortable enough that I was glad to get back out to the car.

"That's the last of it," Gramps said cheerfully. "Let's go home and get cleaned up."

"Cleaned up! What for?"

"Why, to go back to the bazaar, of course. There's a chicken dinner, and then all sorts of activities. You weren't planning on skipping the bazaar, were you?"

"Yeah. As a matter of fact, I was. Why can't I have a sandwich at home?" I asked, but I knew the answer even before he said it. Aunt Mattie would be very hurt if her own family didn't participate.

So we got cleaned up and I wore the new shoes (not the sneakers, but the other ones), and we went back to the church. It was decorated up for a party, with flowers and paper streamers and that kind of stuff. There were booths set up all over the basement, and they were selling all kinds of stuff; and at one end there were long tables where you could sit down to eat.

I suppose that kind of thing might be fun if you went with friends. I saw some kids fooling around who seemed to be having a good time. But none of them came near me. Gramps and I sat and ate fried chicken and mashed potatoes and gravy and salad and hot rolls, and then I had two pieces of apple pie and a slice of chocolate cake. You could eat all you wanted.

Aunt Mattie came over, flushed and smiling. "It's a good turnout, isn't it? The photographer came and took pictures of everything, and we'll have a nice write-up in the paper next week."

I didn't see why they didn't just ask people to donate the same amount of money they'd spend for all this stuff and save all that work, but Gramps said you couldn't operate that way. "In a town the size of this one, everybody supports the community effort, gets something good to eat or pretty to wear, and they all feel they get their money's worth."

"How long do we have to stay?" I wanted to know.

Gramps grinned. "Restless already? Well, why don't you hang around where Mattie can see you for another half-hour or so and then go on home. Maybe by that time she'll be so busy she won't notice you're gone."

So I did. They had games to play, but they were stupid, like throwing a ball at bottles on a shelf and pitching pennies into ash trays. Stuff like that. I bought a fancy apron for Aunt Mattie's birthday, which was in October, and some used comic books I hadn't read before.

The Hopes were there but C.B. couldn't run around and do anything because she was busy taking care of Toddy while her sister sold homemade candy. I wasn't sure I wanted to be with C.B., anyway; some of the guys would be in my class at school and maybe it would be better if I didn't get too chummy with a girl before I got acquainted with them.

The Fowlers were there, too. I ducked around a booth full of potted plants so Mrs. Fowler wouldn't see me. I didn't want to hear what she thought of my dog. Actually, there were so many people that I didn't see how Aunt Mattie could tell whether I was there or not.

I looked around for Gramps and found him playing checkers with an old man he introduced as Teddy Bear. That was really his name; Gramps told me about him afterward. I'd have hated to be *him* and going to a new school.

"I'm going to cut out, now," I said, and Gramps nodded.

"I won't tell on you, boy. I'll probably have to stay until this is all over and the mess is cleaned up. Don't wait up for us."

It wasn't late. The sun was getting low, but it was plenty light yet. I walked home, feeling as if I were the only person in the whole town who wasn't at the bazaar. I saw hardly anyone else going through town.

Funny thing, I thought. Dad wanted me to get to

know kids, but all the ones I'd seen here, except for C.B., didn't act as if they wanted to know me. The only friendly ones were the old people, Gramps's age. I could have met old people without coming to Indian Lake and going to school.

I expected Leroy to come running to meet me, but there was no sign of him.

"Hey, Leroy!" I yelled and waited, but nothing happened.

I walked on down to the lake, wondering uneasily if he were getting into some sort of trouble again. The Fowler place was dark, but there were lights upstairs in the Hope house. I called Leroy again and listened. All I heard was C.B.'s cat, Marcella. It came out of the dusk and rubbed against my legs, making cat-noises.

Which probably meant that Leroy wasn't around anywhere; Marcella took to the trees or went under the porch when he showed up.

The screen door opened, and C.B. came out of the house. "That you, Danny?"

"Yeah. I'm looking for Leroy. He hasn't had supper."

"You're late, so he's probably out stealing something," she said. She came down the steps, licking an ice cream cone. "We had to bring Toddy home because he was getting fussy. I thought you'd stay until it was all over."

"What for? I don't know anybody there. And

the kids don't seem much interested in me . . ."

She nodded and bit the top off the ice cream. "I know. I wish I could go back to my own school."

I had my own wishes, but I knew it wouldn't do any good to talk about them. "I hope you're wrong about Leroy getting into trouble. It wouldn't take much more and Aunt Mattie would insist on getting rid of him."

"You want me to help you look for him?" It was getting dark now, but we could still see to walk along the edge of the lake. We called and called, but Leroy didn't come.

There were lights on at the old Miller cottage, so we didn't go close to it. I told C.B. how Mr. Royce acted when he saw me in town.

"Quick slipped into his car, like he didn't want me to see him. He's not very friendly."

We turned around and headed back. "No. And dogs usually know if people don't like them, so Leroy wouldn't hang around there. Maybe he's off in the woods chasing a rabbit or something."

"In the dark?"

Neither of us knew if dogs chased rabbits in the dark or not. Anyway, by the time we got home, Leroy hadn't showed up. C.B. went back in her house, and I went on to mine. Gramps had just come home; he was bringing in a bunch of stuff Aunt Mattie had bought at the bazaar.

"Didn't she come home with you?" I asked. I'd worked up an appetite, walking on the beach, and I cut a piece of apple pie and poured a glass of milk to go with it. C.B. had reminded me of ice cream, so I put a couple of scoops of chocolate on the pie; there wasn't any vanilla left.

"No, Mattie never leaves until everything is cleaned up, and that'll be a few hours yet. Aggie Kirk will bring her home. I think I'll have some of that pie, too."

He cut a little sliver, and we ate sitting at the kitchen table. I kept listening for Leroy, thinking he'd surely show up soon, but he didn't.

When Aunt Mattie did come home, it was obvious she was really tired, but she was all keyed up. She was carrying still more stuff. Four pies and a box of home-made cookies and half a chocolate cake.

"This was left over, and I couldn't see it go to waste," she said. "We can freeze it."

"Way Danny eats, you won't need to," Gramps said. "He'll clean out the lot of it in twenty-four hours."

"And then be sick," Aunt Mattie said, but I could see she didn't have her mind on that at all. "Guess what, Dad?"

"What am I guessing about?" he wanted to know. He looked at me and shook his head. "Now she thinks I'm a mind reader!"

"I had the most interesting offer tonight. Of course I can't accept it, but it was awfully nice of them to think of me."

"I'm *not* a mind reader, you know," Gramps said. "What in tarnation are you talking about?"

"Aggie's sister, you know, Clara? Well, she came up to me when they were getting ready to leave the church, and she asked if I'd be interested in going with their mother, old Mrs. Whipple, to Florida! Can you imagine?"

"Guess I'll have to imagine," Gramps said dryly. "The way you're dragging it out and leaving out all the crucial information. Why would they want you to go with Mrs. Whipple to Florida?"

She put all the baked goods on the table. The half-cake was right in front of me, three layers and chocolate frosting between each layer, and walnut halves on top. I wondered if I could just taste it before she put it in the freezer.

"She's going to a reunion. Or, I should say, she wants to go. But she's eighty-seven, and they don't think she ought to go alone. She's never flown before. Of course the flying isn't any problem, but the airports are; an old lady in those big, busy places could get lost or frightened. Anyway, this is a reunion of her college graduating class, and there are only twenty-two members still alive. She really wants to attend, but neither Aggie nor Clara can get away right now.

Clara is getting ready for school to open in a week, and Aggie's daughter's expecting her first baby any day now and she's promised to be around for that."

"So, they want you to go instead? Why don't you? You've never been to Florida. I should think you'd enjoy it."

Nobody was paying any attention to me. I cut off a slice of the cake, slowly, and bit into it.

"I would enjoy it," Aunt Mattie said. She was putting on the kettle for tea water. "Only how can I leave?"

"Why can't you? You think Danny and I can't shift for ourselves for . . . how long would you be gone? A week, two weeks? I've cooked my own meals and washed my own duds many a time, daughter. I can do it again. And with Danny here, and Leroy, I couldn't get lonesome. Not in a week or so."

Aunt Mattie stood there in the middle of the kitchen, looking at each of us in turn with bright eyes that didn't even notice I was eating chocolate cake. "It would only be for a week. Do you really think I could go? They'd pay my expenses, of course, but I thought with Danny getting ready to start school and everything . . ."

"So what's to getting ready for school?" I asked. "We've already got clothes and shoes. What else is there to do?"

"You don't have to be here to send him off the first

day," Gramps told her. "We can set the alarm and get him up on time, and he's big enough to go by himself, for pete's sake. Why don't you call Clara and tell her you'll be glad to go with her mother. Chance of a lifetime; you'd be a fool to pass it up!"

We could tell she really wanted to go, yet she hesitated. "How do I know you won't get into trouble while I'm gone?"

"Well, now, we couldn't hardly guarantee the house won't get struck by lightning or that Danny won't fall out of a tree and break an arm, but I'm not totally senile yet, Mattie. I can handle an emergency all right, I think." Gramps sounded a bit testy.

"It isn't that I think you're incompetent," Mattie protested. "It's only that—well, things seem to *happen* to you."

"Not likely your being here or going will make a particle of difference, one way or the other," Gramps said. "You call Clara and tell her you'll go. Danny and I will make out fine, won't we, Danny?"

He winked at me, and I nodded.

I didn't know that the things that were going to "happen" had already begun.

8

Leroy was still missing on Sunday morning. It wasn't until we came home from church (and that was another shock, that I was expected to get up early on Sundays and go to *church*) that I had a chance to look for Leroy again. And then I didn't have to look. Because while I was changing out of my good clothes and back into jeans, I heard him.

Whining, all excited, on the front porch, his nose pushed against my window screen.

"Leroy!" I yelled. I'd begun to be worried something bad might have happened to him, but there he was, big as a moose, wagging his tail and grinning at me. I didn't even put my shoes on but ran out to let him into the house.

He acted as if nothing had happened, poking his nose into my hand to see if I had anything to eat. I got out his dog food and filled his dish, and he ate as if he was starved.

Gramps came into the kitchen. He'd gotten into more comfortable clothes right away, too. "Well, decided to come home, did he? Where you been, boy?"

Leroy wagged his tail but didn't stop eating. Gramps ran a hand over the big head, then looked at his hand. "Where the deuce has he been? Look at that. Got straw or something on him. I hope he didn't get into anybody's barn and bother their livestock."

I looked at him in alarm. "Are there farms close by, Gramps?"

"None real close, nearest would be three-four miles. But that's no distance for a dog." He suddenly squatted and lifted one of Leroy's massive paws. "Been in oil, too. See that? Matted the hair between his pads. Motor oil, smells like. Confounded animal. If anybody comes and complains about him, we're going to have to tie him up or get rid of him."

I swallowed around the lump in my throat. "We wouldn't have to—get rid of him, would we, Gramps?"

He shot me a look of understanding. "Well, I hope not, but we can't have a dog that bothers the neighbors. For one thing, most farmers won't put up with it; somebody'll take a shot at him. He'd be better off tied up than having that happen."

I looked at Leroy, crunching dog food with teeth

that could certainly do a lot of damage if he wanted them to. "He'd never be happy tied up."

"Probably not. But he better stick closer to home and stay out of people's yards and houses then." Gramps stood up. "How long before dinner, Mattie?"

Aunt Mattie came in tying on her apron. "Half an hour. All I have to do is make the gravy and a salad. Danny, you want to set the table for me?"

Well, anyway, I thought, Leroy was back and he was OK for now. At least I hoped he was. If he'd been in trouble, no doubt we'd hear about it before long.

But nobody came to the house to complain. We had dinner, and I had to choose between pie and cake for dessert because Aunt Mattie thought two desserts was too much. I didn't mention how many I'd had the night before. Right after dinner she called her friend Clara, and they made arrangements for her to fly to Florida with Clara's mother.

I could tell Gramps looked forward to being alone. "She's a good woman, Mattie is, but she fusses too much," he told me.

She sure did. She went around telling us, "While I'm gone be sure to defrost the refrigerator," and "do the laundry" and "don't wash that in hot water" and "eat up the pot roast" and I don't know what all. Some of the things she even told us several times, until Gramps reminded her that once was enough.

I escaped onto the beach as soon as I could, but

there was nothing in particular to do. The Hopes had gone somewhere, I guessed, because everything was closed up. The Fowlers were home; I saw them out washing their car. But I thought I'd better stay away from them.

I wasn't in the mood to meet the Royces, either, so I walked the other direction around the lake, toward town. There was a long stretch where there weren't any houses, and then a few summer cottages, and then I came to the town itself. It looked different from the lake side; there was a little park, and some people were having a picnic. Nobody paid any attention to Leroy and me.

We kept on going, on across the public beach. It was late in the season, but there were some kids swimming. They looked at me, but none of them said "Hi" or anything. After a while I came to the beach in front of the Lodge. I wasn't sure if it was private or not, but there was no one around so I kept on walking.

It looked like a nice place to stay. Dad would have liked it, I thought. Big and rustic and comfortable looking. There were boats the guests could use, but they were all drawn up on the shore, and it looked as if they were going to be put away for the winter. Once Dad and I were at a place where we had a boat that belonged to our cabin, and we went fishing and rowing around the lake every day while we were there.

I could see the winter stretching ahead of me, with nothing to do. Dad and Aunt Mattie had taken it for granted that I'd make friends my own age as soon as school started, but what if I didn't? What if the most exciting thing I got to do was walk along the beach with Leroy?

Beyond the Lodge were a few more summer cottages. Leroy went tearing off up a path into the woods. I called him, but he didn't come back. Mindful of Gramps's warning, I went after him.

The path came out on a gravel road like the one that went past our place. There was no sign of Leroy, only a few rural mailboxes with painted-on names so old I couldn't tell what they said. There was a woman in a yellow dress stooping to peer into one of them.

I didn't make much noise moving up to her because I was still on the grass beside the road. "Excuse me, but did you see a big dog go past here?" I said when I was a few yards from the woman.

She slammed the mailbox shut and straightened up as if she'd been shot. When she turned toward me, I saw that it was Mrs. Trentwood, the lady who owned the Lodge. For a minute I would have sworn she looked terrified, and then she put a hand on her chest and gave a nervous laugh.

"Oh! It's Danny Minden, isn't it? You startled me!"

"Have you seen my dog? He came up that path

ahead of me a few minutes ago."

She shook her head. "No. No, I didn't see him. What are you doing way out here?"

"Just walking. I hope that darned dog isn't getting into somebody's garbage."

"There's no one living out here anymore," she said. "They've all gone back to the city for the winter. The places are all closed up, so I wouldn't think he could hurt anything."

I hoped she was right. "Well, I guess I might as well go back this way and hope he finds me," I said.

She stood there beside the old mailboxes, breathing as if she'd been running. I had the funny feeling that I ought to offer to help her, but what sense did that make? If she needed help she'd say so, wouldn't she?

I heard a bark up ahead that sounded like Leroy, and sure enough, there he was. He'd chased a cat up a tall gatepost and was standing there trying to persuade it to come down. He was almost big enough to reach it, and the cat was so scared its fur was puffed up like crazy.

"Come on, you dope, that cat isn't going to play with you," I said and grabbed his collar and hauled him off. When I looked back, the cat was still on top of the post, and Mrs. Trentwood was still standing beside the mailboxes, watching me.

It didn't occur to me until I came up even with the Lodge to wonder what she'd been doing back there.

Because there was a great big mailbox right in front of the building with the name INDIAN LAKE LODGE painted on it.

Now why would a nice lady like Mrs. Trentwood be peeking into someone else's mailbox? Particularly when she'd told me all the people who lived out there had gone back to the city? If there was no one living beyond the Lodge, it didn't seem as if the mailman would even go out past those boxes until next summer.

We walked home through town. There were people around, and they looked at me, but nobody said anything. Maybe small towns were friendly when everybody knew everybody else; but if you were a stranger, I didn't see where they were any improvement over big cities.

About halfway home I heard a car coming and turned around. It was Mr. Royce's old beat-up station wagon, but he never even slowed down when I waved. He went right on past as if he didn't see me.

"And a nice day to you, too," I muttered. It wouldn't have hurt him to offer me a ride, since he had to go right past our place. Leroy looked after him and barked as if he agreed with me.

Aunt Mattie didn't leave until Tuesday, and you wouldn't believe what she thought had to be done beforehand. The floors had to be scrubbed and waxed, and all the laundry done just as if Gramps and I weren't smart enough to operate the washer and dryer. (Dad and I always did the laundry together, if we stayed somewhere there wasn't a valet service.) And she made up casseroles to put in the freezer for us, and she kept making up notes to put on the front of the refrigerator, and reminding us to do things.

Gramps finally exploded. "For crying out loud, woman, go pack your stuff and get out of here! You're not going to be gone for months, and we can take care of things! You're wearing us out!"

Contrite, she stopped in the middle of explaining how the oven worked. "I'm sorry. I am being foolish, aren't I? It's only that I'm excited, and I feel guilty about leaving you alone—"

"Well, you are being foolish, and I'm glad you're excited, and there's no reason to feel guilty. Just don't spoil it for *us* by going on this way. Go and have a good time, and we'll surprise you by being in perfectly good condition when you come home."

Aggie Kirk and her sister Clara came in the afternoon to pick her up and drive her and their mother to the airport. I got kissed four times, as did Gramps, and Aunt Mattie even had a word to say about Leroy.

"Take care of that dog. Don't let him get into trouble. And don't either of *you* get into trouble."

"Go," Gramps said. "Go, Mattie. Have a good time." He was still shaking his head after they'd disappeared down the road. "Poor Mattie. She shouldn't have retired from teaching school. She doesn't have enough to do anymore, so it makes her fussy."

"Do you remember my mother?" I asked.

"Of course I remember your mother! What a question!"

"Was she like Aunt Mattie?"

"Lorraine? No, not much. Oh, they were both good, warm, loving women. But no, Lorraine wasn't like Mattie. She always liked traveling with your father, wherever he went. Mattie likes to take an occasional trip, but she's a homebody at heart. Too bad your mother died so young. It's been lonely for you and your dad, both."

"I suppose it was for Dad. I know he misses her. But we got along fine, Dad and me. I think I'll write him a letter," I said and went into my room to do it. I tried to write only the good things or the interesting ones, but it was hard. I wanted to plead with him to let me join him, at least when he came back to the United States, because he wouldn't be in Ireland for the whole school year. But I didn't. I'd try not to be a crybaby about staying here for this year. But I was sure going to try to talk him into taking me back with him as soon as school was out next spring!

When the weekly paper came, I was glad Aunt Mattie wasn't there to see it. It gave me a funny feeling to see all those pictures of Leroy and me. I was sort of proud, but embarrassed, too, and I wondered if the other kids would react the way Paul Engstrom had. Resentful, because the story built me up as a hero. I hadn't said those things about myself, but maybe that wouldn't matter, they'd still think I was showing off.

I wasn't sure whether to clip the page out and send it to Dad or not. Finally I did. Gramps chuckled and said he'd better get an extra copy of the paper, seeing it had all our pictures in it, the whole family. Because there was a story on the church bazaar and Aunt Mattie, too.

The first two days Aunt Mattie was gone absolutely nothing happened. We got up and ate and took care of the things that needed to be done, and then Leroy and I would swim with C.B. or read. It was nice and peaceful, and Gramps didn't care how many servings of dessert I ate or what time I went to bed. Not that there was much to stay up for, but at least it was nice to set my own schedule.

The third day Gramps went into town to play cards with Teddy Bear and Paddy O'Hara and Bill Allenduff. I went along to the library, because I was running out of reading material. Gramps read a lot, only he liked mostly mysteries and westerns. He never read any science fiction, but he said they had some at the library.

We didn't take Leroy because we were going in the car and Gramps said he'd get hair all over the seats. Leroy didn't especially want to stay home; he sat on the porch looking forlorn.

I found a bunch of books I hadn't read. It was a little library, but they let me take as many books as I wanted as soon as I told them who I was. I didn't even have to have a card.

When I got home, I called Leroy, but he didn't come bounding around the corner of the house. I went into the kitchen and then I stopped. My fingers went slack on the books and they slid onto the floor.

I never saw such a mess in my life as that kitchen was.

9

My first thought was, *Aunt Mattie will kill us.*

It was a disaster area.

I hardly knew where to look first.

The potted plants on the windowsill by the door had been spilled off and lay broken on the floor, the dirt scattered around them.

The curtains on that window had been pulled halfway off the rod, and there was a dirty smear and a tear in one corner.

The cushions were out of the rockers, and one of the chairs had overturned. When it fell, it had brought down a lamp; the shade and the bulb were smashed. We had done the laundry that morning, and Gramps had folded it and left it stacked on a chair. I was going to put it away when I got home, but now it was on the floor and there were dog footprints all over it, and dirt from the potted plants mixed in with it.

And all over everything was what looked like about a ton of feathers. Pillow feathers, I decided after the first sick reaction had simmered down to something I could control. Sure enough, I found what was left of the pillows from my bed; they'd been ripped apart by what had to be dog teeth.

Oh, boy. Aunt Mattie was going to be furious.

I began to get pretty mad myself. "Leroy? What got into you, you rotten dog? How come you made such a mess? Do you *want* to get kicked out of here?"

There was no answer, of course. Leroy wasn't there. I went in my room and looked, half-expecting he'd be sleeping on my bed. He wasn't.

Of course, the pillows were gone, and there were more dirty tracks on the bedspread. They looked like chocolate tracks.

Then I remembered that I'd left a glass on the nightstand, one that had had chocolate milk in it the night before. It was knocked over, and that blasted dog had walked through the puddle it made and then jumped onto the bed. I groaned.

It would be quite a while before Gramps came home (and was I ever glad Aunt Mattie was in Florida!), but I wasn't sure how much improvement I could make before anyone saw the place. There wasn't much I could do about fixing the broken pots and the damaged plants, nor the torn curtain, nor the smashed lamp. The laundry I could rewash; it didn't seem to be torn or anything, just dirty.

But I figured the first thing I'd better do was find Leroy. If he went on such a rampage at home, what might he do somewhere else?

I started around the edge of the lake, calling his name. It was hard not to sound mad enough to kill him, but I knew he'd never come if he thought I was going to punish him, so I tried.

"Hey, Leroy! Here, boy!" I yelled, but there was no sign of him. And then I came across the front of the Fowler place, and there on the beach was a red sandal. It had been ripped into three pieces.

I said some of the words my dad says when he's really mad, like if some of his film gets ruined or something; but when I finished, the sandal was still there, in three pieces.

I picked it up and carried it along with me, thinking maybe the best thing would be to bury it. Mrs. Fowler was mad enough already, and what good would it do for her to see what had happened to her shoe?

I kept on calling that darn fool dog, trying to pretend I still liked him, and wondering what I was going to do when I caught up with him. It would be a miracle if Aunt Mattie let us keep him now, even if she didn't find out about him destroying the neighbors' property.

C.B. was sitting on the edge of her dock, kicking her feet in the water, eating an apple. "What's he done now?" she called.

I held up the bits of the red sandal. "It belonged to Mrs. Fowler. But this isn't the half of it. You should see our house."

She slid off the dock, winced, and reached around to pull a splinter out of her shorts. "What did he do to your house?"

"Come and see," I said grimly. What the heck, Leroy was nowhere in sight, probably because I wasn't controlling my anger well enough; he could tell by my voice I wanted to take a stick to him. "Aunt Mattie's going to kill him—and probably me, too."

C.B. stood with her mouth open when she saw the mess. "Oh, gosh! He's never done anything like this before, has he?"

"He'd never have lasted ten minutes if he had. I can't imagine what got into him."

"Maybe he was upset because you all went off and left him," C.B. suggested. "And he was bored, so he played with the pillows, and while he was swinging them around he accidentally knocked over the other stuff."

"Sure. Explain that to Aunt Mattie and see how understanding she is."

She sighed. "I guess you're right. Mother wouldn't be very understanding, either. You want me to help you clean up the mess?"

"I'll take any help I can get," I said, but I wasn't very cheerful about it. There were too many things we couldn't fix.

We got out the vacuum cleaner, and I started sucking up feathers. C.B. shook her head over all the footprints on the laundry, but she thought they would wash out. We weren't sure about the chocolate on the bedspread, but she put that in the machine, too.

There wasn't much we could do about the lamp but sweep up the broken glass and carry it and the shade out to the trash can. C.B. thought she could save the plants, and we found some more pots out in the tool shed to put them in.

It took us quite a while. When we'd done the best we could, C.B. surveyed the kitchen with a sigh. "If I were you, the next time I leave him alone, I'd leave him outdoors," she said.

I stared at her. "I did. He was sitting on the back porch when we drove away."

"Then how did he get inside? Can he open the screen door by himself?"

I got a funny, tight feeling in my chest. "Not that I know of. No, he always sits outside and whines to come in, and Gramps or I open the door for him."

"It *was* Leroy, wasn't it?" she asked slowly, her face screwed up in thought.

"You saw the size of those footprints on the laundry."

She nodded. "I never saw any dog but Leroy who had feet that big. But unless he's learned to open the door . . ." She turned and pushed at the screen.

It had one of those catches on it that held it shut, and I was sure that had been holding it when we left. We were careful about screens because Aunt Mattie hated flies and we all hated mosquitoes.

And it opened *out*. Leroy might have been able to *push* it open, but he certainly couldn't have *pulled* it from the outside.

We looked at each other, and C.B. said what we were both thinking. "Somebody had to let him in."

I looked around the kitchen. It didn't look too bad anymore, if you discounted the smashed lamp and the torn curtain, but I pictured it the way it had been a few hours ago.

"If Leroy was *chasing* somebody, he might have caused all that damage."

"If he caught them, there ought to be blood some-where," C.B. said. "And I can't imagine anyone being able to keep away from him. He looks big and awk-ward, but Leroy is fast."

It was a puzzle, all right, and one we couldn't solve.

I had started out by being furious with that darned dog. But once I began thinking that maybe some person had been in the kitchen with him, I was worried instead. Where was Leroy? Had something happened to him?

"Nobody could carry him away," C.B. pointed out. "He weighs as much as a horse; even a man would have trouble lifting him or even dragging him on a rope, if he didn't want to go. So he must have left on his own four feet."

There was some logic in that, and maybe it ought to have made me feel better. It didn't. I was definitely uneasy.

"It's too bad there aren't any neighbors close enough to see your house," C.B. said. "Maybe somebody could have seen something, if they weren't all gone for the winter. Do you think we should go looking for Leroy, Danny?"

I didn't know what else to do. We were careful when we went outside; we looked for clues to what had happened. But there was grass around the house, and it didn't show any footprints or anything. And beyond the grass there was sand. The only place that would show prints was right down by the water where it was damp.

That part of the sand was as smooth and unblemished as if no one had ever passed that way.

"Seems to me I've spent an awful lot of time walking up and down around this lake looking for that dog," I said. "Maybe I won't have to much longer;

when Aunt Mattie sees what happened in her kitchen, she'll probably insist that we get rid of him."

The Fowlers were on the beach in front of their cottage, playing badminton with a net on poles stuck in the sand. They stopped when they saw us.

"Hi," Jerry Fowler said. "Want to play?"

I shook my head. "No, I have to find my dog. Have you seen him?"

"Not today. He isn't in trouble again, is he?" They both looked at me intently.

"I just have to find him," I evaded. Maybe they'd find out eventually what had happened, so I didn't want to lie, but I didn't want to admit what a mess he'd made, either.

C.B. and I went on down the beach. Eventually we came to Marcella up in a tree; she meowed when she saw C.B.

"Do you think Leroy's been chasing her?"

C.B. shrugged. "She climbs trees sometimes just because she wants to. Come here, kitty. Come, Marcella."

But Marcella wouldn't come down. She backed up along the limb, so we gave up and left her there.

We kept calling Leroy, but he didn't come. Maybe Gramps was right. If we kept him, we'd have to tie him up. I swallowed past a painful lump, thinking of a free-running dog like Leroy being kept on a chain. He wouldn't be able to run on the beach anymore;

nobody could keep up with him to take him on a leash. I could picture him, his hair flying, ears flopping back, his tongue lolling happily. It would break his heart if he couldn't run.

I was hoping the Royces wouldn't be home, but they were. The station wagon was in the driveway. Deciding not to go any closer, I whistled, thinking maybe Leroy could hear me and Mr. Royce wouldn't.

Suddenly a radio came on, real loud, and then Mr. Royce stepped to the front door. He looked at us as if he was angry, although unless Leroy had been there, I didn't see why he should be.

"Don't your folks ever keep you kids to home?" he demanded.

"We're looking for my dog," I said.

"Well, we ain't got any dogs here. We rented this place because it was supposed to be private and quiet, and with you brats running back and forth, it ain't either one." He turned around and slammed the door shut behind him.

"Nice guy, isn't he?" C.B. said dryly. "If they need quiet so much, why don't they turn the radio down?"

"Yeah. They can probably hear it over at the Lodge across the lake," I agreed. "You think there's any use in going on as far as the apple orchard?"

By this time we didn't really think anything was worthwhile. We decided as long as we'd come this far we might as well keep on going, though. But we didn't find Leroy, nor any trace of him.

We got back just about the time Gramps came home. He got out of the car and came toward us, grinning. "Wasn't a bad day. I won six cents. Don't tell your Aunt Mattie that; she doesn't approve of gambling."

"Is six cents gambling?" C.B. asked. "Playing for pennies?"

"It's all any of us can afford. And it makes it more interesting."

I opened my mouth to tell him what had happened to the kitchen, but it was too late. He was already through the doorway.

"Holy catfish!" He surveyed the room in disbelief. "What happened?"

We both started talking at once. We told him we'd fixed what we could and cleaned up the feathers. And we told him we guessed maybe someone had been there who let Leroy into the house, unless he'd suddenly learned to open the screen door.

"Do you think anything's missing?" C.B. asked. "Maybe someone came in to steal something, and Leroy chased him out."

"If somebody came as a thief, why would he let that ox of a dog in with him?" Gramps wanted to know.

We didn't have any answers to that. We stood

around while Gramps checked through the house.

"Nothing missing that I can see. Silverware is still there. We don't have all that much that's valuable, I guess. Maybe you shouldn't have cleaned up the mess; the sheriff might have been able to find some clues, if there was somebody in here."

"We didn't think of it until we'd finished cleaning up," I confessed. "That someone had to have let Leroy in, I mean. I was just mad that he tore it all up this way."

"Glad Mattie's in Florida," Gramps muttered. "Maybe I better call Ben Newton, just tell him what happened here. Funny things going on in Indian Lake these days."

The sheriff said he'd come out and take a look, he wasn't busy right then. Though it was getting close to supper time, C.B. didn't go home. She wanted to know what Ben Newton would think of the situation.

When he came, the sheriff asked a lot of questions and looked around at everything. He walked around the house and up and down the driveway and then down onto the beach, but he didn't find any more clues than we had. Until he stopped at the corner of the tool shed.

There was some loose dirt there, in front of the door, where Aunt Mattie had spilled some of the dirt she had for her plants. Ben Newton squatted down and looked at that dirt.

"You find something?" Gramps asked.

The sheriff looked around at Gramps's feet. "What size shoes you wear, Charlie?"

"Nine and a half. If you found a footprint, it's not mine. I haven't been in the tool shed in a couple of weeks, not since it rained last."

"Two prints here. A big one and a little one." He looked around at C.B. and me.

"The little one's mine, I think," C.B. said. She turned over her foot so we could see the pattern on the bottom of her sneaker. It matched the smaller print in the dirt.

"The other one's—oh, I'd say about a size ten. Bigger than Danny's, too. Couldn't be Mattie's, could it?"

Gramps made a strangling sound. "Glad Mattie didn't hear you ask that. She prides herself on her dainty feet. No, it's not Mattie's. Man's shoe, wouldn't you say?"

Sheriff Newton made grunting noises when he was thinking. "Nothing remarkable about it except that there's a crack across the ball of the foot. I'll just measure it to be sure of the size, but I doubt we're going to catch up with whoever made it unless he goes around making more prints. Don't know if we could even say a crime has been committed, to tell you the truth. Some damage done in your house, but nothing missing, you say. And the damage could have

141

been done by your own dog."

"He never did anything like this before, though," I said. "And if there was a man in the house, well, maybe he did something to make Leroy get all excited."

Ben Newton stood up. "Could be. We'll be lucky if we find out, though. Let me know if you turn up anything else that looks interesting. I don't know what this town is coming to. More crime here lately than I can ever remember. People breaking into houses, robbing banks." He shook his head. "We're going to have to start locking our doors like the city folks do. In fact, they're already doing that over at the Lodge. Met the manager in town this morning, said Mrs. Trentwood told him to put new and better locks on every door in the place. Nobody used to have to lock doors in Indian Lake."

"Was there a robbery at the Lodge, too?" I asked.

"Not that I know of. If there was, they didn't report it. Well, nothing more I can do here. Keep your eyes open."

Gramps walked over to the police car with him. C.B. looked down at the footprints in the dirt. I could tell she felt bad because she hadn't seen that footprint herself; but of course when she came out to the shed for new pots, we were still thinking Leroy was responsible for all the mess. We weren't looking for clues. I told her that.

She gave me a weak grin. "Still, I wasn't very observant. What do you suppose he was out here for? It looks as if there *was* a man, and he was in the tool shed as well as in the kitchen."

Gramps was walking toward the house; he called out to us before I could answer C.B. "I'll get started with something to eat, Danny!"

I nodded and stood looking after him. "There are some really funny things going on around here. Thieves who don't steal anything. The guys who broke into that empty house didn't take anything or do any damage either. And why would they put new locks on every door at the Lodge unless something happened? Locks are expensive."

"Maybe Mrs. Trentwood was scared because of the other break-ins," C.B. suggested.

"She doesn't know about this one yet; it just happened. And if she was scared by the other one, that happened days ago. Why wait until today to change the locks?" That reminded me of something else. "Another funny thing happened, too." I told her about Mrs. Trentwood's acting so startled when I met her on the road, and how she was peeking into someone else's mailbox. "She doesn't seem to be the sort of person who'd do that. It's illegal, isn't it, to monkey around with somebody else's mailbox?"

I'd already told her about Mrs. Trentwood's running over the fire hydrant, and then going home without doing her errands.

"She's been upset and nervous every time I've seen her. Is she usually that way?"

"I don't think so. I don't know her very well, but my mother does. She's very nice. She donates money to the fund for fireworks on the Fourth of July; and when there was a fire last spring, she let the people whose house burned stay at the Lodge for nothing until they could have repairs done."

She had the door of the shed open and was looking around inside. It was sort of dark because there were only two windows and they hadn't been washed in a long time. "Whoever he was, he must have had a reason for coming out here. It looks like just junk. A lawnmower, and tools, and an old bedspring."

I saw the dangling light bulb and reached up and pulled the string. "There, now maybe we can see." It was the way she said, though, just a lot of junk. There was a box of old canning jars in one corner, and some of them were broken. I started to turn away when C.B. gave a little cry.

"Danny, look! Those have been broken recently, see how the glass is scattered on top of the lawn-mower? And look at this!" She swooped on one of the jars and picked it up, holding it so I could see it better. It was a quart jar with the top broken off, and there was a stain around the broken edge.

"It's blood!" she said dramatically.

For a minute I thought she was letting her imagination run away with her, as Aunt Mattie would have said. But then I took a closer look.

"Maybe you're right. Is there any more?"

When we looked very closely, we found it, several drops splattered around on the edge of the box that held the jars and a couple of drops on top of the lawnmower.

"Somebody cut himself, maybe when he fell into those jars and smashed them."

C.B.'s green eyes were big and round. "Let's see if there's a spot that isn't covered with dust, where he took something!"

We didn't find anything like that, however. When Gramps called me in for supper, we gave up. But we were both excited, because something very peculiar was going on, and before C.B. went home we decided to find out what it was.

Gramps and I talked about it while we ate. He didn't hold out much hope we'd ever know who the intruder was or what he wanted, and mostly he was glad Aunt Mattie wasn't there because she'd have been upset. He thought he could get a new shade for the lamp and tell her it was a surprise homecoming present, and maybe he'd talk to Aggie Kirk and ask her to pick out some new curtains to replace the torn one.

Then he pushed back his chair and stood up. "You

mind doing the dishes tonight, boy? My bird in the cage is almost done, and Teddy Bear asked me to bring it in for him to see. He wants to try to make one like it for his great-grandson." His eyes twinkled. "I don't think he can make one as good as mine, but maybe he can satisfy a three-year-old who doesn't know any better."

So I cleared the table—after I ate the last piece of cake because it didn't seem worthwhile to put it away—and did the dishes. I kept listening for Leroy, but he didn't come. The more I thought about it, the more ominous it seemed. The blood on the broken glass, and Leroy disappearing.

Odd things kept occurring to me. Like the nervous way Mrs. Trentwood acted when she was going to park in front of the sheriff's office but ran into the hydrant, instead. Had she been going to report something to him? And then chickened out and went back home without doing it? Had there been a crime out at the Lodge, and was she, for some reason, afraid to tell Ben Newton? But if that was why she was putting new locks on all her doors, why had she waited so long to do it? And why had a nice respectable middle-aged lady been snooping in someone else's mailbox? And most important, was there any chance all those things had any connection with an intruder in our kitchen and Leroy's disappearance?

Maybe it was too soon to worry about Leroy.

Maybe there wasn't anything wrong at all, he was only lolloping through the woods chasing a rabbit. But Leroy was a dog who liked his meals, and he had a good inner clock that told him when it was mealtime. That was the part that made me so uneasy. If he *could* come home, wouldn't he do it?

And if he couldn't come home, was he hurt? Or even dead?

All I knew for sure was I had to find him. Maybe he got into a lot of trouble, and he ate like a horse, and he wasn't popular with the neighbors. But he was the first dog I'd ever had, and I liked Leroy.

I remembered the load of laundry C.B. had put in the dryer, and I got the stuff out and began to fold it on the kitchen table. I hoped all that chocolate had come out of the bedspread.

It had, but when I got to the pillow cases I found that all the marks hadn't washed out of one of those. When I smoothed it out, I stared at a dog footprint right in between two embroidered yellow daisies. And I got that funny, tight feeling in my chest again.

Because, although it was clearly a dog's footprint, it wasn't Leroy's. It was a little tiny print, but as clear as it could be because the dog that had made it had stepped in oil or something that had left a bad stain and a perfect footprint.

I rolled it up and forgot about the rest of the laundry. I had to show that print to somebody right away, and Gramps might not be back for hours. I took off through the edge of the woods for the Hope house.

C.B. was feeding Marcella in a fancy dish on the porch. She came down beside me, though, when I spread the pillowcase out on the steps so she could see it.

"That's not Leroy's! There was another dog in your house!"

"Sure looks like it. Who around here has a dog as little as the one that made this print?"

"Nobody. We don't have anyone but Marcella, and it's bigger than her foot. The Fowlers don't have any pets, and that's all of us living on this side of the lake. Except for those Royces, and they don't have any pets, either."

"But there was a little dog around this afternoon. It was in the house with Leroy."

She ran her tongue over her lips. "Maybe whoever owned the dog went into the house after it."

"He had to let it in, in the first place, didn't he? Unless it could open doors itself."

She screwed up her face the way she did when she was thinking hard. "The little dog and Leroy were playing, and the owner of the little dog tried to put Leroy in the house, but they both got in, and he chased the little one trying to catch it?"

"And wrecked the house and just walked out and

left the mess? And then what happened to Leroy? Where is he?"

"I don't think that was Leroy's blood in the tool shed," she said.

"No. I don't either. Maybe the guy was chasing the dogs in there, too, or trying to shut Leroy in there or something, and he slipped and fell in the canning jars and hurt himself. But Leroy isn't shut in, at least not at home, so where is he?"

She blinked her eyes. "Maybe he's shut in somewhere else. He's nosy, maybe he followed this man home and accidentally got shut in somewhere."

"Accidentally?"

After a minute she shook her head. "No, that doesn't sound likely, does it?"

We walked down to the dock and sat on it, talking, for quite a while. I kept hoping old Leroy would come loping along the beach, chasing a bird, but he didn't.

It was still quite light when I had the idea. "Let's go over to the Lodge and talk to Mrs. Trentwood."

"What for? What's she got to do with Leroy? We know for sure she wasn't the one who got in and messed up your house!"

"Yeah. But she's mixed up in something peculiar, I'm sure she is. And how many mysteries can there be in one little town like this? If I guessed right about her coming to town that day to talk to the sheriff and then getting scared when she ran over the hydrant and going away without talking to him, maybe it's connected with *our* mystery. What have we got to lose? I can't just sit here without doing anything to find Leroy, and maybe she can give us a clue."

C.B. thought it all sounded farfetched, although she was as intrigued as I was over what Mrs. Trentwood's mystery might be. We decided to take the Hopes's boat and row across the lake rather than walk all the way around, so she got the oars and I pushed us off the beach.

It was a nice evening, warm and quiet. The lake was smooth, and when I trailed a hand in the water, it was warm, too. C.B. rowed first, because it was her boat and she was used to it, while I sat in the bow and made sure we were aimed at the Lodge. And then when she got tired, I took over. We didn't talk, except to say if we got off course. I would have enjoyed it, if I hadn't been so worried about Leroy.

When we finally nudged the beach on the other side of the lake, C.B. sprang out. I was glad to ship the oars; I'd been wondering if my arms would hold out until we got there. Rowing was fun, but it was hard work.

We were right in front of the Lodge. We tied up to one of the pilings on the dock and started up the bank toward a man who was watching us with what appeared to be displeasure.

10

"That's Mr. Hagen. He's the manager," C.B. muttered under her breath. "They don't like town kids to trespass over here."

"We aren't trespassing. We've come to see Mrs. Trentwood," I told her, but I had to admit the way that guy was looking at us made me nervous.

At least Mr. Hagen wasn't rude like Mr. Royce. He waited until we walked right up to him, and then he said rather coolly, "What can I do for you?"

C.B. looked at me. I cleared my throat. "We'd like to see Mrs. Trentwood, please."

"I'm sorry. Mrs. Trentwood is indisposed."

"What's that mean?" C.B. hissed at me.

"It means either she's sick or she doesn't want to see us. But since he hasn't asked her, he can't know whether she wants to see us or not. Is she sick?"

I thought he turned sort of pink. "The Lodge is closed. We can't help you, I'm afraid."

"We didn't ask *you* to help us," C.B. said reasonably. "We asked to see Mrs. Trentwood. She's still here, isn't she?"

He looked at the building as if he expected her to be looking out one of the upstairs windows. "Yes. She's still here. But she does not want to see anyone. Take my word for it."

I knew for sure that I had to talk to her, then, but I didn't quite see how to go about it. He was standing between me and the door that opened onto the terrace, and even if I got inside, I didn't know how to find Mrs. Trentwood.

"Would you ask her, please? If she'll talk to Danny Minden? It's important."

"Mrs. Trentwood is resting," he said. "I couldn't possibly disturb her."

"Well, when she comes down," C.B. insisted, "will you tell her we were here? That we want to talk to her?"

Annoyance twisted Mr. Hagen's mouth, but he was still polite. I suppose being the manager of a hotel, he made a habit of it. "May I say what you want to talk to her *about*?"

I hesitated. "Tell her it's about a—a mystery."

His eyebrows twitched. "A mystery. Very well I'll give her your message."

We stood there for a minute more, until I realized he wasn't going to do anything right then. There was nothing we could do, so we turned around and went back toward the beach.

"If the Lodge is closed," C.B. said as soon as we here out of his hearing, "why is *he* still here? Or any of them? They usually pack up and go as soon as their last guests leave. Within a couple of days, anyway."

"Mrs. Trentwood is still here," I said with growing conviction, "because there is something fishy going on. And I'm going to find out what it is."

"How?" C.B. wanted to know.

We had reached the boat, but I didn't untie it. "I don't know. But for starters, let's go look at that mailbox she was looking into. See if there's anything there to give us a clue."

Mr. Hagen had gone inside. Otherwise he might have stopped us from going on around the lake toward that path Leroy and I had taken to the road. When we got into the woods, it was pretty dark, and it occurred to us that maybe we'd have to row home across a black lake.

"No problem, though," C.B. assured me. "We can aim at the lights from our house, so we can't get lost."

When we came out of the woods onto the road, it was dusk. We could see where we were, though. "It was that mailbox," I said, pointing. "The one on this end, in that batch of four boxes."

She leaned forward to read the name on it. "P.T. Patrick. I don't know them, but I've heard their name. They didn't even come to the lake this year; they're traveling in Europe instead. Why would Mrs. Trentwood be snooping around in their mailbox? The mailman wouldn't even have put mail into it."

I didn't think so, either, and I don't even know why I pulled it open. It was just as illegal for me to do it as it was for Mrs. Trentwood. I didn't expect to find anything.

But there *was* something in it. A folded piece of paper. I stared at it until C.B. wanted to know what was the matter, and then I took it out. I unfolded it and held it close enough so we could read it in the fading light. I heard C.B. swallow.

It wasn't addressed to anyone, and there was no stamp or envelope, so it hadn't come through the mail. The printing was done in pencil, and it was hard to see. I read it out loud.

"Leave the money in the mailbox at midnight. Don't come back here and don't call the cops and Mac will be returned to you tomorrow."

There was no signature.

"Is it what I think it is?" C.B. spoke in a whisper, looking nervously over her shoulder. There was nothing in sight but dusty road and woods.

"It's a ransom note. It's what she was looking for, a ransom note. No wonder she jumped when I spoke to her! Who's Mac?"

She shook her head. "I don't know. I didn't think she had any kids. She used to have a husband, but he died a long time ago. What are we going to do?"

"We're going to take the note back to the Lodge and manage to talk to Mrs. Trentwood," I said. "I'll bet she's not asleep at all; she's just upset and waiting for it to get dark so she can come and look in the box again."

"A kidnapping! I don't believe it," C.B. said.

I believed it. That would explain a couple of things. Like why she'd been so nervous she'd driven into the fire hydrant. Maybe she was coming to tell the sheriff about the kidnapping, although she'd probably been warned not to, and then she was so afraid she went home without daring to do it. It would explain why she'd been crying when I delivered the pies. And it was one darned good reason why a nice lady would be looking in someone else's mailbox and didn't feel well enough to want to talk to anyone now, and why she was still at the Lodge after it was time to have closed it up for the winter.

I refolded the paper and stuck it in my shirt pocket. It was going to be dark before long, and I didn't want to be out by those mailboxes when the light was gone. We trotted along the edge of the road, not seeing anybody, but both of us worried that someone might have been watching. If they were, though, they stayed hidden; we didn't see anybody.

The Lodge already looked deserted, with no cars in the parking area and only one light on, deep inside somewhere. We walked up to the front door and tried it.

"Are we going to just walk in?" C.B. whispered.

"If it's unlocked. I'm not going to take a chance on Mr. Hagen's throwing us out. This is too important. And I don't want to tell him about it, because maybe he doesn't know, and maybe Mrs. Trentwood doesn't want anyone to know."

I turned the knob, and the door eased silently open. The light we saw came from the dining area beyond the lobby, and we could hear voices. We moved quietly, wondering which way to go to find Mrs. Trentwood.

"Maybe they're all eating," C.B. said, still in a whisper. "Let's sneak up and see."

There were four people in the big dining room, but none of them was Mrs. Trentwood. A fat woman in a black dress was heaping food on her plate, and she spoke crossly.

"Well, when is she going to send us home, I'd like to know? We're already a week late, and what are we staying here for? There's no customers, nobody to cook for but her. And she's not eating enough to make it worthwhile to turn on the stove! What's going on?"

"She hasn't informed me," Mr. Hagen said. "If you want to leave, go ahead. I can manage the cooking as long as she needs me. But don't expect to come back next year if you leave her in the lurch now, Mrs. Petty. There is such a thing as loyalty, even if you don't know what the problem is. Anyone can look at Mrs. Trentwood and see that she's in great distress. So go, if you want to."

The fat woman was eating, and she swallowed quickly before she answered. "Oh, I won't leave her if she needs me. She's a good woman to work for. But my family is expecting me home, and I don't know what to tell them."

"Tell them you've been delayed," Mr. Hagen said.

I tugged on C.B.'s sleeve. "Come on. She must be upstairs."

We didn't dare turn on any lights, but we found our way to the second floor all right. Mr. Hagen had glanced up at the windows overlooking the lake when he spoke of her, so I hoped Mrs. Trentwood's room would be on that floor and side of the building. Maybe there would be lights on so we could tell.

If there were, we couldn't see them, because there were no cracks under the doors. It was practically pitch black up there, so we turned on a hall light, hoping no one downstairs would see it.

And then we found Mrs. Trentwood because she opened a door and came toward us.

She looked terrible. She stopped when she saw us, and stood in the middle of the hallway.

"Mrs. Trentwood, we wanted to talk to you," C.B. said quickly.

Her mouth moved, but at first she couldn't seem to make the words. And then she said, "Mr. Hagen said you'd been here, that you wanted to talk to me about a—a mystery."

"I don't know if your mystery is connected to *our* mystery," I said, "but maybe it is. We need help, and maybe you do, too."

She was very white. She looked past us, so that we looked over our shoulders, too, and then she said, "Come into my sitting room where no one can hear us."

She had a nice room, with a couch and a stereo and lots of books and things. There was a door open into a bedroom beyond. She sank into a chair as if she were collapsing, and we sat opposite her on the couch.

"Maybe you'd better tell me what you're talking about," she said.

I handed her the note and watched her grow even more pale when she read it.

"Where did you get this?"

"Out of that mailbox down the road. It's a ransom note, isn't it?"

For a minute she didn't say anything. Tears formed in her eyes.

"Yes."

"Who's Mac?"

"You've figured it all out," she said, and one of the tears spilled over. She brushed at it with her fingers.

"We figured out somebody named Mac has been kidnapped and is being held for ransom. Do they want a lot of money to bring him back?"

She nodded. "Yes. Quite a lot. I'm willing to pay it, you see. But I've been waiting and waiting for the ransom note, and it wasn't there. I thought they'd leave one right away, after they told me the message would be in that old mailbox. But nothing happened."

"Who's Mac?" C.B. wanted to know.

"Mac is my dog." Mrs. Trentwood turned to the table beside her chair and picked up a photograph to hand us. It was a cute little dog with blond hair that fell into his eyes. I guess my astonishment must have been written all over me.

"People kidnapped your *dog* for ransom?"

"MacDuff isn't an ordinary dog," she said. She waved her hand toward the fireplace opposite us, and I saw a row of trophies along the mantel. "He's a pedigreed Silky Terrier, and he's very valuable. The puppies he fathers are worth several hundred dollars apiece. But he's more than that to me."

She groped for a handkerchief. "MacDuff is all the family I have. I had a little girl once, but she died, and then my husband was killed in an accident. So all I have is MacDuff. His real name is Sir Angus MacDuff of Kentsbridge, but we call him MacDuff for short."

"He's a dog," C.B. said, and when she looked at me I knew what she was thinking. "Is he real little, so his footprint would only be about this big around?"

She made a circle with her thumb and first finger. Mrs. Trentwood forgot to wipe her eyes. "Yes. Why? Do you know where he is?"

"I think maybe we know where he *was*," I said slowly. "I think he was in our house this afternoon."

She cried out and got up from her chair then, all excited. It took a little while to explain it to her, even with both of us talking at once.

"Does he chew on shoes?" C.B. asked.

"Oh, my, yes! I have to hide them from him, he loves to tear shoes all to pieces!"

"Does he like hot dogs?" I asked, thinking of the ones missing from the Fowlers' kitchen.

"Oh, he likes most anything except dog food. Even," she gulped, trying to smile, "peanut butter sandwiches."

I looked at C.B. "Maybe it wasn't Leroy that stole our lunch. Maybe it was MacDuff."

"But if he was kidnapped, he wouldn't have been running around loose, would he? How long has he been missing?"

"Since the second." She looked at the calendar standing on her desk. "All that time I've been waiting for some word!"

"Did you report it to the police?"

She shook her head. "No. I thought about it, and I *wanted* to do it; but the first note, the one that came through the mail in my own box marked *personal* and with no return address, it said not to call the police if I wanted to see MacDuff alive. I didn't dare tell anyone, not even Mr. Hagen, because I knew he would insist on calling in the sheriff. But if it meant risking MacDuff's life, I couldn't do it, you see. What's this about your lunch?"

We explained. "There was a lot of food missing that day. Our lunch, and hot dogs from our neighbors. We blamed it on Leroy, but he ate the same as always, so maybe it wasn't him. Maybe MacDuff was loose. I know if he was kidnapped you wouldn't expect him to be running around loose, stealing food or chewing up shoes. But maybe he got away from the kidnappers for a while; maybe that's why you didn't get the ransom note as soon as you expected, because they had to catch him again first. And there was sure a little dog in our house this afternoon because we found his footprint on a pillowcase. If the kidnapper was trying to catch him and tore all around our kitchen wrecking the place because MacDuff didn't want to be caught, and Leroy was helping him—well, that would account for the mess we found, wouldn't it?"

We all stared at each other, and there was almost electricity in the air from our excitement.

"But if MacDuff got loose, especially if it was *twice*," C.B. said, "wouldn't he have just come home? I mean, all he had to do was run halfway around the lake. Leroy does that practically every day."

I hadn't thought of that. Before I had more than a glimmer of disappointment, though, Mrs. Trentwood was shaking her head. "No, I don't think so. That's been worrying me, because MacDuff wouldn't take kindly to being confined by strangers, especially if they tried to make him eat dog food. Yet if he got away, he might easily be lost and I'd never find him again. He's an indoor dog, you see, a show dog, and he's never allowed out of doors except on a leash. He would ruin his coat if he ran through the woods. He was lost in the city, once, only a few blocks from home, but he couldn't find his way back to the apartment. I had to offer a hundred dollar reward, and someone brought him back to me. So I know he doesn't have enough of a sense of direction to find his way all alone in strange territory."

"Then your mystery *is* connected to our mystery," I said slowly. I was beginning to see some of the implications, and I didn't like them very much. "If it was MacDuff at our place, then Leroy was there, too, when the kidnapper was chasing him. Now Leroy's missing. Leroy isn't a valuable dog, at least not to anybody but us, and we don't have any money to pay a ransom. They might not . . ." The words stuck in my throat, but I managed to get them out. ". . . might not worry about keeping Leroy alive. If he was a big nuisance, and he probably would be, they might . . . shoot him, or something."

C.B. looked shocked. "Oh, they wouldn't do that! Besides, someone would hear the shot and wonder about it! They wouldn't take the risk, do you think?"

I remembered how big a pest Leroy could be. Kidnappers probably didn't have much patience about such things.

"I think we'd better go tell Ben Newton about this," I said slowly. "Before anything worse happens. If he knows that footprint was made by a kidnapper and not just a bum that got into our house, he'll think it's a more important case and he'll solve it."

"No," Mrs. Trentwood said. "No, we can't do that. In a town the size of this one, everyone learns everyone else's business so fast; and if the kidnapper knew I went to the police, he might . . . hurt MacDuff. I can't take that chance."

"But we have to do something," C.B. pointed out. "Even if you pay the ransom money and get MacDuff back, what about Leroy? We have to find Danny's dog, too."

For a minute no one said anything. I swallowed and cleared my throat. "I guess we'll just have to find them ourselves," I said.

"How would we go about that?" Mrs. Trentwood

said. She'd stopped crying, and she sounded hopeful.

"Yes, Danny," C.B. echoed. "How would we go about it?"

"I'll think of something," I promised. And I told them the clues we had to work on.

11

"When Leroy was gone before, he came home with hay all over him and oil on his feet. And that footprint that didn't come off the pillowcase in the wash, that was made because there was oil on MacDuff's foot. So maybe they were together in the same place."

"But where?"

"Well, people usually keep hay in barns or sheds. And oil drips out of cars or gets spilled in garages."

"There must be dozens of garages and barns and sheds around here," C.B. protested.

"Yeah. But if MacDuff isn't a country dog, and the kidnapper was after him, maybe he didn't go very far. In fact, seeing that he turned up several times—like when Mrs. Fowler's sandal was chewed up and my sneaker was missing, and the hot dogs disappeared— well, maybe he's being kept somewhere pretty close to us. So it could be worthwhile to look in the barns and sheds and garages on our side of the lake."

Mrs. Trentwood was pale again. "It might be very dangerous to do that. Maybe I'd better just put the money in the mailbox tonight, the way he said, and then wait for him to bring MacDuff home."

"That's OK for MacDuff, if the guy keeps his word. I have my doubts about a kidnapper's code of honor, though. And if he has Leroy or has done anything to him, well, *I* want to call in the sheriff. So isn't the best solution to see what we can find? You can go ahead and put the ransom money in the mailbox. Maybe we ought to wait and watch it after midnight, to see who turns up to get it."

Mrs. Trentwood turned so white I thought she was going to faint and fall off her chair. "Oh, we couldn't do that! What if he caught us watching? Who knows what he would do? He's bold, you know. He apparently picked a lock and got into the Lodge, and then he took MacDuff right out of my rooms! He made terrible threats." She twisted her handkerchief in her hands. "I wish there was someone to ask for advice, but I can't think of anyone who wouldn't simply insist on calling in the police. And I can't risk that. The most important thing is getting MacDuff back—and your dog, too, of course."

I could see that we could sit there talking all night and not get any further than we were right then. I stood up. "Well, I think we'd better go back to our own side of the lake and see what we can do. You put the money in the mailbox, and if the kidnapper brings your dog back, great. If he doesn't, or if he doesn't turn Leroy loose, too, we'll be trying to find them. And maybe we can do that before you pay him the money. Once we get MacDuff back, you won't object to calling in the sheriff, will you?"

She didn't leave any doubt in our minds about that. If the kidnapper were drawn and quartered, it would be too good for him, she said.

"If we find them before midnight, we'll call you," C.B. told her. "And if we don't call, you go ahead and put the money in the mailbox."

We agreed on that, then, and Mrs. Trentwood walked downstairs with us. Mr. Hagen came out of the dining room, and I could see that he was surprised and upset that we'd gotten into the Lodge.

"It's perfectly all right, Mr. Hagen," Mrs. Trentwood said. "And if these children return or call me on the telephone, I want to be notified at once."

He looked at us as if we were something that had crawled out from under a rock, but he nodded his head. "Very well, Mrs. Trentwood."

"He was polite, but he doesn't like us," I said to C.B. on our way down to the boat. "I wonder if he's in on it, somehow."

"Mr. Hagen? Why do you think that?"

"Well, I don't really. But someone had to know that Mrs. Trentwood has a lot of money and that she's crazy about that dog. Most people wouldn't pay a fortune to get a dog back, even if they had a fortune to begin with, would they? And who would know better than Mr. Hagen how attached she is to the dog? And how come he doesn't realize her dog is missing? He must know that's what's making her so upset."

C.B. climbed into the boat, and I untied the rope and jumped in after her. It was so dark that if there hadn't been a moon we might have had trouble finding our boat, but she was right about our being able to aim for the lights of the Hope house. We took turns rowing, and this time I wasn't so tired. Maybe it was because I was so busy thinking about what might have happened to Leroy that I forgot the strain on my muscles.

We could see there were no lights on at our house. Gramps hadn't come back yet. I was sort of hoping he had; I thought Gramps was the kind of adult you could confide in without him thinking you were having a hare-brained idea. He wouldn't go to pieces no matter what you told him, not like Aunt Mattie.

"Are we going to go looking now? Right away?" C.B. asked.

"Well, I am. Will your folks be upset if you don't come home?"

"Maybe the smart thing to do would be to go inside and tell them good night and get a book out of the living room. I'll go upstairs, and they'll think I've gone to bed to read. Then I'll climb out on the roof of the porch and down that big tree. I've done that before, it's easy."

"OK. I'll go home and get a flashlight and leave a note for Gramps. I'll meet you back here in ten minutes," I said.

I guess I was still hoping Leroy might show up, but he wasn't there when I got home. The doors were all unlocked and nothing was disturbed. I found the flashlight, all right, a neat one with a little chain on one end of it that could be fastened around a belt loop so I'd have both hands free if I needed them.

I got out paper and a pencil, but I couldn't think what to write to Gramps. It was all so complicated. Finally I just wrote, "I'm looking for Leroy," and left it at that. Gramps wouldn't be excited about that. I still thought it would be smart to call in Ben Newton, but Mrs. Trentwood had practically made us promise we wouldn't do that until she got her dog back. I understood how she felt; I'd probably feel the same way if it were Leroy.

I didn't use the flashlight going back to C.B.'s house. It was plenty dark under the trees, but with the moonlight on the water there was no trouble seeing where the edge of the lake was. I found her waiting at the end of the dock, licking her arm.

"What are you doing?"

"I slid faster than I expected and scraped off some skin. It's OK, though, I had a tetanus shot in July when I stepped on a nail. Where are we going to start?"

"Well, we've already been through our shed. So let's work our way along this whole side of the lake and investigate every outbuilding we come to and all the vacant houses where anybody could hide a dog."

She glanced toward the lights in the Fowlers' cottage. "Even the Fowlers'?"

"Sure. I don't think *they* have anything to do with this, but we won't skip anything. We'll be really thorough."

So we were. The Fowlers only had a shed, smaller than ours, and just as cluttered and dusty. There weren't any dogs in it, nor any sign there ever had been.

The Hopes' garage had two cars in it and nobody ever closed the doors, so we let that go with a cursory check with the flashlight in the corners. Marcella's amber eyes blazed at us from under one of the cars.

"We probably scared a mouse she was chasing," C.B. observed.

We moved on along the shore, checking all the windows and doors of the empty cottages and all the outbuildings. We found oil on the floors in two garages and musty old hay in one shed, but never the two in the same building and no sign of any dogs.

At the Bernard place, where we knew someone had broken in, we finally found something unexpected.

The sheriff had nailed the boards back over the window when he was finished checking the house out. Now two of them had been pried off again and leaned against the siding.

We were standing there, staring, when we heard footsteps inside the house. Not dog footsteps, but human ones.

I felt a lump rise in my throat, and I couldn't even make my fingers work to turn off the light. I was still standing there when the face appeared in the opening between the remaining boards. With C.B. rigid beside me, I waited for whoever it was to speak.

12

My heart was hammering so hard my chest hurt. C.B. sucked in a scared breath and then seemed to stop breathing altogether, and I didn't blame her.

The first thing I realized about the face in the opening above us was that it was terrified.

The second thing was that it was Paul Engstrom.

Relief made me almost drop the flashlight. It also made me rude. "What the heck are you doing in there?" I demanded.

Paul leaned forward to see us better. "Who is it? That Minden kid?" His fear evaporated and was replaced with indignation. "What are you doing messing around here?"

"Are you the one who broke into this place before when Mrs. Kirk called the police?" C.B. asked. She appeared to be breathing again now.

"No. I didn't have anything to do with that." He turned sideways, so his shoulders would fit through the place where the boards had been pried off, and eased a leg over the windowsill. He had a flashlight, too, but his wasn't turned on. "What business is it of yours, anyway?"

He slid to the ground and looked at us defiantly, brushing the smudges off his hands onto his pants.

"It's everybody's business if you're mixed up in something illegal," C.B. said. "It's our duty to report it to the sheriff."

Alarm stopped the movements of his hands. "Hey, cut that out! I'm not doing anything illegal!"

"Breaking and entering is illegal. Isn't it, Danny? And maybe that's not all you're doing. Maybe you're hiding a couple of dogs in there, too!"

This time all he appeared to be was bewildered. "You're crazy! What would I be doing with dogs in a deserted house?" For a minute I think he really believed we *were* crazy and wondered if we were dangerous.

"Then explain what you were doing in there. At night. Without a light. Alone. You are alone, aren't you?"

"Yeah, I'm alone. And the bulb burned out on my flashlight after I got in there. Look, what's going on?"

By this time I didn't think he had anything to do with the kidnapping, but I wasn't positive. "You tell us," I said. "What's going on? You don't live here, and you pulled the boards off the window and went in someone else's house. How come?"

Resentment burned in his face. Fat chance I was ever going to have this guy for a friend, I thought. All Dad's ideas about me and my peers were going right down the drain, and school hadn't even started yet.

"You going to report me?"

"Depends," C.B. said, before I could answer. "What were you doing in there?"

"I wasn't stealing anything." He spread his hands to show that he had nothing on him but the flashlight, but there was a bulge in the pocket of his jeans. C.B. pointed at it.

"What's that?"

I couldn't be sure, for the light was dim, but I thought he flushed.

"Nothing important."

That time we simply stood there, looking at him, until he jammed a hand in the pocket and brought out the object. I brought up the light to focus on it.

"A bowling trophy?" It was so little, I wondered if it was a booby prize or something. "Is it yours?"

"No," C.B. said. "It belongs to Mr. Bernard. He has a bunch of them. I remember seeing them on the dresser when we were here before. You *are* stealing!"

She was going to make points with the local kids, too.

"I'm not stealing it. I'm going to return it," Paul said defensively. "After I use it to prove I was really here. Nobody will ever know it was gone; I'll bring it back tomorrow."

We digested that. "Why do you have to prove you were here? Who you proving it to?"

"It's an initiation stunt. You know, to get into the Secret Club," he said, looking at me. "I have to prove I had the guts to come down here alone and go in the house at night, and this is how I prove it, by taking back something they'll know belongs here. It has Mr. Bernard's name on it."

I guessed he was telling the truth. What other reason would he have for doing such a dumb thing? I shrugged. "OK. We won't report you, not if you're going to put it back."

Paul stuck the little trophy back in his pocket. "What are you guys doing here?" He looked closer at C.B., decided she was a girl, but didn't change the way he addressed us. "Maybe I'm the one who ought to report *you*. What were *you* doing?"

"Investigating," C.B. said. "We can't tell you any more than that; it's confidential."

I could have told her that that was a stupid way to turn off the guy's curiosity. She should have made up some silly lie. Now all she'd done was intrigue him. You never intrigue anybody if you don't want them to ask questions.

Paul's eyes narrowed. "Investigating what?"

I poked C.B. in the ribs with my elbow and she gave me an injured look. "I wasn't going to tell him. I know it's a secret."

"Turn about is fair play," Paul said. "I told *you* the truth."

"It isn't really our secret to tell," I said. "It involves someone else who made us promise—"

"*I* didn't promise anybody anything. How do I know you're not up to something crooked? Huh? Why shouldn't I be the one to report to the cops?"

It was a stalemate. I didn't know if he'd really go to the cops or not. I was inclined to doubt it, because then they'd want to know what *he'd* been doing out here. On the other hand, I didn't want to risk poor MacDuff, either.

I licked my lips. C.B. was watching me to see what I'd decide. Now was a fine time to be keeping her mouth shut, I thought, after she'd already blown it by making him curious.

"If I tell you, you have to promise not to tell anyone else. Not until . . . well, until it's all over."

"Until what's all over?" He slapped at a mosquito on his forehead, but not as if he were really aware of it.

"Look. Maybe we could use some help. Three-heads-are-better-than-two stuff. It could be danger-ous, and if you don't want to help, that's OK. But regardless of what you do, you have to give us your word of honor you won't tell anybody—not anybody —until we agree that you can."

By that time I think he'd have agreed to anything. His mouth was open, waiting to hear what it was.

"This better be good," he said.

"Your word of honor," I insisted.

"OK. Word of honor."

So we told him.

He didn't believe a word of it.

I couldn't have cared less, if I'd been sure he wouldn't go back to town and tell the kids in the Secret Club everything we'd said. If the word got back to the kidnapper before we could rescue Mac-Duff and (I hoped) Leroy, we might never get them back. Not alive, anyway. And we'd promised Mrs. Trentwood.

"Look. How can we prove it to you? If we had a telephone you could call Mrs. Trentwood and she'd tell you it's the truth. Only she'd be real upset because she's afraid this guy will kill her dog if she doesn't pay him the money and let him get away with it. We can't be sure he'll do what he says even if she *does* pay him the money, but she has to do it before midnight, so we have to hurry. What time is it?"

Neither of us had a watch, but Paul did. He held it under the flashlight. "Quarter to ten. Listen, is this on the level? Some guy actually kidnapped a dog for ransom?"

"It's true," I assured him earnestly. "And we don't have much time. We were going to check out all the empty houses, barns, garages, and sheds on this side of the lake. Did you see any sign that anyone had been in the Bernard house with a dog?"

"I wasn't looking for anything like that." He was beginning to be convinced. "You want to go back inside and see?"

So we did. C.B. went first and I handed the flashlight up to her, and then Paul and I followed.

It was spookier at night than it had been in the daytime. We moved around, looking for something chewed up (there was an old pair of slippers under a bed, but they were intact) or dog droppings. There was nothing.

When C.B. shrieked it raised the hair right up on the back of my neck. At the very least, I expected to turn around and see an axe-murderer coming out of a closet.

Judging by Paul's face, he was feeling the same way. "What did you do that for?" he demanded.

"I just remembered! When we were here before, Danny, remember? We found dog food in the kitchen!"

"Lots of people leave dog food in their cabins through the winter," Paul said. "Just like they leave the rest of their canned goods. As long as it doesn't freeze, it's OK next year."

"But the Bernards never had a dog." She was moving toward the dinky kitchen, and I followed with the light. "See, here it is on the counter. Dog food. Why would there be dog food here when they didn't have a dog?"

"What else is there?" Paul asked. "The Bernards were vegetarians, weren't they? Then how come they bought Spam?" He poked at the can, and then tipped up the sack the stuff had come out of and looked at the grocery sales tag. "Here, shine the light on it."

I looked over his shoulder. The stuff had been bought at a place called Flagg's Market, and Paul's thumb pointed out the date. August 31st. Just before MacDuff disappeared.

"And there wasn't anybody living here in August!" C.B. cried triumphantly.

"Whoever broke in brought this stuff with them. They were going to stay here, but they got scared off because their lights were seen and the sheriff checked them out," I said.

Paul believed us, now. "Holy cow! It must have been the kidnapper! He was really here!"

Suddenly it seemed like the night closed in around us. We were all aware that we were in a deserted house, and that there weren't any close neighbors. My voice sounded hollow.

"They came here before they kidnapped MacDuff. And then they got scared off, so they went somewhere else."

Paul's voice dropped to a whisper. "Where?"

"Maybe," I said, and hoped they didn't notice the tremor when I spoke, "they decided it was too risky to break in a place, so they decided to rent a cottage and look legitimate."

C.B. spun around to look at me. "The Royces?"

"Maybe. It was the day after the cops came out here that Mr. Royce came to look at the Miller place."

"Who's Mr. Royce?"

"A guy who says he doesn't like dogs, and who told us to beat it when we offered him some apples. Maybe he just didn't want us around for fear we'd see something."

"Or hear something," C.B. said. "Remember how they turned the radio up so loud when they knew we were on the beach? Maybe so we wouldn't hear Mac-Duff if he barked! Or Leroy!"

It could have been that way, I thought.

"What are we going to do?" Paul asked, still whispering. When I moved the flashlight, shadows danced around us like ghosts in the rafters.

"We're going to go over to the Miller place and look, aren't we, Danny?" C.B. was looking at me as if she had no doubt about my courage. If it hadn't been for Leroy, it might have been fading by that time. I had a hunch Mr. Royce could be a mean customer.

"Yeah," I agreed. "We're going over there and look. You want to come along?"

For a few seconds Paul wavered, and then he nodded. "OK. I'll go with you."

So we climbed back out of the window and went down to the lakeshore and headed away from home. Far out across the lake we could see the lights of the Lodge; not many of them, but we were sure we could pick out the ones in the suite upstairs where Mrs. Trentwood was waiting. She wouldn't wait much longer for our call, only a little over an hour, and then she'd take the money and put it in the mailbox. I hoped she'd hide in the woods and see who came to get it, but I doubted if she would. She was too scared.

I guess that wouldn't be too fine a word to use for the way I felt, either. The closer we got to the Miller cottage, the tighter my chest felt. I didn't want to use the flashlight, because I remembered how I'd seen Royce's the night they moved in, and we didn't want anyone to spot us.

There were lights in the front part of the house. They had the windows open because it was a warm night, and we could hear the radio playing softly. The station wagon sat in the driveway behind the house. I risked flashing the light under it and saw that it leaked oil; there was a wet, black spot. Was that where Leroy had walked in oil?

We stopped well back under the trees. "What now?" Paul asked.

"Well, maybe we could get close enough to see in

the windows. They don't have the shades drawn."

We hesitated. I guess we were all uneasy about walking up and looking in anyone's window.

"What if they see us and call the cops?"

"If they're the kidnappers, they won't call anybody," I said.

"Have they got guns?" Paul wanted to know.

C.B. made a protesting sound.

"How should we know? We'll have to be really quiet, or they'll hear us. Don't step on sticks or anything that will make a noise."

"How are we going to know where the sticks are, in the dark?"

"Well, just be careful. I'll sneak up on this side, and Paul, you sneak up on the other side. I don't think we can get close enough to see anything in front, not without going up on the porch."

We all agreed the porch was off limits; it would be too easy to get caught. We decided C.B. would stay where she could watch the front door and whistle if anybody came.

"I can imitate a whippoorwill," she said, and demonstrated.

"Do they call at night?" I asked.

None of us knew for sure, but it seemed a better bet than having her yell "Run!" or something. So we left her there and started edging toward the lighted house.

I wished they had the radio turned up more. The music stopped and a newscast came on, but it wasn't enough to cover me if I made much noise. I kept to the shadows under the trees as long as I could, and my heart was pounding so loud I couldn't hear Paul at all.

I eased toward the window, finally, and I knew if anybody looked up when I got close, I was going to be seen. Fortunately the house wasn't very high off the ground; I wouldn't have to climb on anything to see in.

And then when I got there, it was disappointing. Mr. Royce sat with his back to me, smoking a cigarette and drinking something cold out of a can. He kept drumming his fingers on the arm of his chair until the man across the room snapped at him.

"For crying out loud, can't you stop that?"

It was the first time I had a good look at the second man, the one who'd helped Royce move in. He was shorter and stocky, and he had a round face and not much hair except for a fringe over his ears. I didn't see any sign of Mrs. Royce. Maybe she was sick enough to be in bed. Or maybe, I thought with my newly suspicious mind, there wasn't any Mrs. Royce. Maybe he just made her up because it would seem more normal to Aggie Kirk if the cottage was rented by a man and his wife rather than by two men.

I didn't see any sign of a dog, either. What if we

were wrong, and we got caught here, and Royce called the sheriff? How would we explain? Mrs. Trentwood would have to release us from our promise of secrecy.

"Get me another drink, will you?" Royce said, and the stocky man got up and went into the kitchen and came back with another sweating can. Royce popped the top and tipped it up to drink. I could hear him gurgle and wondered that he didn't hear me breathing and turn around to see who was out here. He put up a hand to brush back his hair, and I saw something that held me very still. There was a cut across his right hand, just the way there might have been if he'd slipped and fallen into a carton of canning jars and cut himself on one of them.

The other man moved out of my line of sight, and after a minute Royce yelled out, "Spud! What time is it?"

"Ten after ten. Early yet."

Royce swore and lit another cigarette although he hadn't quite finished the first one. He slapped at a mosquito on his neck. "Lousy screens in this place. Anything smaller than an elephant could get in. Are you sure the clock is right?"

"I'm sure. Hey, did you hear something?"

We all froze and listened. I pushed a hand against my chest as if that could calm my heartbeat, although reason told me they couldn't have heard *that*.

"Nah," Royce said at last. "Just night noises. This place gives me the creeps. I'll be glad when we can get out of here."

Spud moved back into sight, carrying a sandwich with lettuce and meat hanging out the edges. He took an enormous bite and spoke through it. "Yeah. Me too. Listen, you think I ought to go out and look around? Just in case?"

"Go ahead. Can't hurt anything," Royce said.

I started backing away, wishing I could imitate a whippoorwill. I didn't dare cut across the front of the place, because Spud was going out the front door, so I headed toward the back. Too late it occurred to me that I'd have been smart to have scouted around beforehand, so I'd know what was back there. The moonlight didn't penetrate here away from the lake at all, and if I ran into a tree Spud might hear me.

I hoped Paul was retreating, too, and that C.B. could see us moving away. If she did, she'd know why. Right then, I heard her whistle.

Spud heard her, too. I was easing to the rear of the cottage, feeling my way and stepping carefully. His voice was plaintive. "I thought the country was supposed to be quiet and peaceful. Listen to that stupid bird, don't they ever sleep?"

I was afraid C.B. would overdo and make them suspicious, but she didn't.

A low branch whacked me across the forehead,

making my eyes water. I stood still until the pain receded, then went on my way, hands outstretched to avoid another collision.

I heard Spud walk across the porch and down the steps. When he stopped, I did, too. He moved again, going away from me, and I decided if he was going to walk around the house I'd better get further out in the woods so we didn't run into each other. It wasn't any darker there than where I was.

Paul must have melted into the trees because Spud didn't yell or anything. Pretty soon he came around the back and again I stopped, right up against a tree, although I doubted that he could see any better than I could. He was silhouetted against the lighted window on my side of the house, and then he called out.

"Don't see anything. I guess this place just spooks me. I'll be glad to get back to the city."

"Me too," Royce grunted. "What time is it now?"

"Ten minutes later than it was the last time you asked," Spud said, and he sounded annoyed.

By this time I had reached the back of the cottage. For such a little place, it sure took a long time to get around it. I paused, wondering if I dared risk the light. I didn't remember from the times I'd been there in the daylight what the heck was back there.

"Danny?" C.B.'s whisper came out of the darkness so close to me I jumped.

"Yeah. I'm here. Where's Paul?"

He materialized behind her. "Here. Boy, this is nerve-wracking, you know that?"

"You're telling me. C.B., you've been here oftener than I have. Are there outbuildings?"

"A garage with a dirt floor and an old chicken house. I don't remember it ever having chickens in it, but summer before last they kept a goat, and sometimes they shut him in there when they were going away for the day because he could pull up his stake and wander away."

"You think those guys are the kidnappers?" Paul asked. "They seem awfully nervous."

"They would be nervous if they were going to pick up the ransom money in a few hours, wouldn't they? Listen! Did you hear anything? Is he coming back?" I held my breath.

I felt C.B. tugging on my shirt. "Get down! Quick!"

We all dropped to our hands and knees as cautious footsteps came along the side of the house. If he'd stayed on the grass, he'd have taken us by surprise, but his feet crunched on gravel in the driveway.

Oh, boy, I thought, if he's got a light he's going to find us! And even if he hasn't, if he stays close to the house he's going to step on us!

Beside me I heard Paul grunt; there was a soft scuffling sound, and fingers tugged at me again. I moved in response to them, hoping C.B. knew more than I did.

I almost yelped when I hit my head on the side of the back porch steps. I knew then what Paul and C.B. had done; they'd wriggled under the porch through the area where the latticework was falling apart. I followed them, moving backward. One foot hit somebody, and I squeezed myself through the opening just in the nick of time.

It was Spud, and he had a flashlight. He flicked it over the porch steps, only inches from where we were. I saw that my knees had gouged marks in the dirt, but Spud didn't seem to notice. He mumbled something I couldn't understand and went on around the house.

For a long time after he'd gone we crouched, motionless and silent, listening to each other try to breathe inaudibly. That isn't easy when you've just been scared half to death. Finally C.B. squirmed and made a tiny noise.

"Danny? Look what I found."

I moved a hand in her direction and took the can she'd shoved at me. "It's the same size as those dog food cans we found in the Bernard place."

A rustling indicated C.B. was still squirming around. I wasn't surprised when she made a faint, distressed sound, because I smelled it just before she spoke.

"There's been a dog under here not very long ago."

Nobody answered. What was there to say?

We waited a little longer, still not hearing anything. I remembered the night Royce and Spud had moved in, how Leroy had startled them and I'd heard their canned goods falling when they dropped them. This one had rolled under the porch. I was sure it was dog food.

Funny stuff for them to buy, if they didn't have any dogs around.

"Danny, I'm scared! Let's beat it and get the sheriff!" C.B. said.

I had come to the same conclusion myself. It had sounded good, getting out and rescuing MacDuff and Leroy before the ransom was paid, but now that we were almost face-to-face with the kidnappers, I realized how dangerous it could be. I didn't suppose the penalty for kidnapping dogs was the same as for kidnapping people, but it was a crime, and if they were caught they could go to jail for a long time. They might do anything to keep that from happening. I was afraid of what "anything" might include.

I guess they thought I was still holding back about calling in the sheriff, because Paul added his whisper to hers. "She's right. They might shoot us or something! Let's get out of here!"

I started to crawl out of the hole, and that's when I saw the feet. A man's feet, right in front of me.

A minute later, a flashlight was turned into my eyes and a big hand grabbed hold of my shoulder.

"All right, come out of there," Spud said, and he didn't sound friendly. He didn't sound friendly at all.

13

"How many of them are there?" Mr. Royce asked. He sounded nervous and very angry. His adam's apple was bobbing like crazy.

"Only two of us," I said quickly. "Paul and me. We—we didn't mean any harm, it's just an—an initiation stunt."

Spud still had hold of my shoulder, and he shook me the way Leroy would shake an old shoe. "Who are you? What are you doing here?"

I was so busy hoping C.B. had got the message and would stay put that I hardly heard what he said to me. It wasn't until he shook me harder and repeated his questions that they registered. Then Mr. Royce answered the first one before I could get my mouth open.

"It's that Minden kid. The one that's always running up and down the beach. He owns that big dog that's such a blamed nuisance."

"And who's with you? Who else is under there?" Spud turned the flashlight downward, and Paul crawled into the opening, blinking, breathing through his mouth. When my gaze automatically followed the light, I saw Spud's footprint in the dirt, about a size ten shoe with a crack across the wide part of it.

"Never saw that one," Royce said. "Who are you, kid?"

"Paul Engstrom. It's true, we didn't intend to steal anything, nothing like that. It's an initiation stunt." Paul got to his feet and stood in front of the hole. I didn't dare look down to see if C.B. was still hidden.

"What were you doing? How come you're messing around our place?" Spud demanded. He let go of me then, but I didn't have any wild ideas about getting away from him. I didn't have a chance.

"It's to get into the Secret Club," I said and looked at Paul. He nodded vigorously.

"Yeah. To get in, you have to do what they tell you. Like bring back a wheel off the minister's bicycle. Or . . . or a bowling trophy. See?" He tugged at the one in his pocket, then stared at it in dismay. "Oh, criminey, I broke it! Oh, gosh, we aren't supposed to do that! It's just to prove we actually went some place, see? And then we can take it back later."

They were both staring at us with suspicion.

"Where'd you get that? I never saw it here."

"No, sir," Paul agreed immediately. "It came from a house down the road. See, it's got Mr. Bernard's name on it. And we were supposed to get something that could be identified as coming from here."

"Like what?" Spud said.

"Like—like . . ." I tried desperately to remember something I'd seen through that window, something that might have been used to prove we'd been here. "Like that crummy—I mean funny—lampshade in the living room, the one with hand-painted fruit on it."

"How'd you expect to get that, with us sitting there right next to it?" Royce wanted to know.

"We were going to wait until you'd gone to bed," I said.

"Yeah. Almost nobody locks their doors around here," Paul added. "We figured we'd wait until the lights all went out and then sneak in and grab it."

"Well, you figured wrong. We ought to hand you over to the cops," Spud snarled.

Under the circumstances, it was hard not to hope that they would. I wasn't afraid of the sheriff, but I was sure afraid of these guys. I didn't say it, though. It wouldn't have been natural to agree to something like that.

"You could be lying," Spud accused. "Whatta you think, Royce? They lying?"

"Why would we be lying?" Paul protested. "We were just fooling around, and when we heard you coming out we got scared and hid. That's all. If you let us go, we won't come back. Honest."

"If they *are* lying," Royce said, and you could almost watch him thinking it out as he talked, "we don't want them talking to anybody before—not tonight."

"Yeah. You know what happens to kids who go where they don't belong? Bad things, sometimes. Real bad."

"We won't bother you anymore," I said.

"You bet you won't. Because you won't have a chance. Whatta you think, Royce? Maybe we should lock them up for a few hours."

"It's still not eleven o'clock," Royce said. "Wouldn't hurt 'em to be locked up for an hour or so. Until—" He didn't finish that sentence.

"You can't lock us up!" Paul told them. "You can be arrested for that sort of thing, it's the same as—"

I kicked him in the leg and he shut up. I didn't want him to say *kidnapping*. I didn't want them to guess that we knew what they were up to.

"You should have thought of that before you came snooping around. Come on, you can cool your heels for a while," Spud said. He grabbed each of us by an arm and hustled us toward the garage. His flashlight banged me in the head when he shoved me ahead of him, and I wondered what had happened to the light

I'd brought from home. I hoped C.B. had found it and would have sense enough to rescue us or go for help, one or the other.

"Somebody might come looking for them," Royce said. He sounded uneasy.

"Well, if they do, we'll tell them the kids needed a lesson. In there you go, buddies, and think about your sins for a while!"

He practically threw us into the garage. It was a ramshackle building with only a dirt floor; I smelled the oil that had leaked out of somebody's car, but I didn't get a chance to see much before Spud had closed the door and the light was gone.

Paul and I knocked into each other, getting to our feet. Paul hammered on the inside of the door and yelled. "Hey! You let us out of here! Let us out!"

In the silence when he paused we heard Spud say, "There, let's see them get out of that. Listen, you think maybe we ought to go now? Just in case? She might have been there already."

"We said midnight," Royce answered. They weren't talking very loud, but we could make out the words, all right. "We better wait until then, anyway. We don't want anybody to notice us hanging around."

"You don't think these kids found out, somehow?"

"Nah, how would they? *She* wouldn't tell a couple of kids. What good would that do? She wants—"

They were moving away, and we couldn't make out the rest of it.

I pressed my face against a crack between the boards, but all I could see was their light, bobbing toward the house.

Paul was right beside me, breathing heavily. "They really did it, didn't they? That has to be what they're talking about, they really did kidnap Mrs. Trentwood's dog! You think they'll keep us here very long?"

"At least until they pick up the ransom money." Actually, I wouldn't have been surprised if they took the money and left town without ever coming back here to let us out or do anything else. "C.B.'s still out there somewhere. Maybe she can get us out of here."

"Yeah, I hope so. Say, that was pretty smart, you making them think there were only two of us. At least *she's* still loose."

For a while we wondered, though, because after Royce and Spud were gone we didn't hear anthing for a long time. At least it seemed like a long time.

Paul began to move around, feeling his way along the inside wall. "Is the door they locked the only one there is?"

"I didn't get much of a look at anything," I admitted. "I don't know."

"Hey, I forgot! I've got some matches!" I heard him feeling around for something to strike them on.

"My mom had me burn the trash this afternoon, and I have some matches left! Let's see what this place is like."

He didn't have very many matches, but there were enough to show us only one small window (nailed shut and with panes too small to get through even if we smashed the glass). No other door. There were odds and ends of junk like you find in old garages, none of it useful.

"I think this may be where Leroy was," I said, sounding as subdued as I felt. "He had oil on his feet and bits of hay in his hair. There's hay on the floor here. I'll bet he followed them and they shut him up in here."

"How did he get out, then? Maybe we can get out the same way."

We found a place where it looked as if a dog might have tunneled under the wall, but somebody had filled in the dirt and put cement blocks against it on the other side. If we had to, we could dig it out again, but it would take quite a while.

"C.B. will do something to get us out easier than that," I said.

"Maybe she ran for home and to get help. She hasn't made any noise. I wish she'd hurry up," Paul agreed.

And just then we heard her whisper. "Danny? You in there?"

We pressed against the door and whispered back.

"You sure they're gone?" I asked, and Paul pleaded, "Get us out of here!"

"They're inside. I waited until I was sure. They're getting ready to leave. I heard one of them say they might as well drink the rest of the six-pack because otherwise it would go to waste."

"Can you unlock this door?"

"I don't know yet. I haven't found the lock and I don't dare turn on the light. Wait!" We heard the rattle of the hasp, and she grunted, tugging on it, and a minute later the door creaked open. "Lucky they didn't have a padlock, they just shoved a stick through it."

We hurried out and pulled the door shut behind us. Boy, did it feel good to be free again! I glanced toward the back of the house; there was a dim glow through the kitchen window, but no sign of either Spud or Royce.

"Come on, let's get out of here," Paul said. He was already moving.

"Wait a minute! We came out here to rescue the dogs, and we haven't even found them yet!"

"We could get the sheriff and let him rescue them," Paul suggested.

"But if they take MacDuff with them, Mrs. Trentwood might never get him back," C.B. said. "Kidnappers don't always turn their victims loose the way they promise. Danny's right, the important thing is to rescue MacDuff and Leroy, if they're here, and then we'll get the sheriff."

There was only one place to look, and that was the shed. I didn't really have much hope that Leroy was in there, because I thought he'd have been barking his head off when he heard my voice. But we looked, anyway.

It had the same kind of device as the garage for keeping it locked, but this time we hit a snag. There was a shiny new padlock.

"Leroy? You there?" I asked, but there was no answering whine.

"We're not going to get that off," Paul said when we examined the lock. "Let's see if there's any other way into the place."

C.B. stood guard, watching the house, while Paul and I circled the shed. At the back, where no one from the cottage could see us, we found a window. Not only that, but when we climbed on a woodpile to reach it, we discovered that it could be opened.

There were nails holding it in. While Paul held the flashlight, I worked them loose, and we lifted the window out. Immediately, we heard a low growl.

My heart jumped, but I realized at once it wasn't Leroy. It was much too small a growl for Leroy.

The flashlight swung around the interior of the little shack, and there he was.

MacDuff. A little blond fluffy dog, with hair hanging in his eyes and a red leather collar almost buried in matted fur.

He didn't look much like his picture. He was dirty and snarled, and he didn't seem especially friendly.

"Here, Mac!" I called softly. "Here, MacDuff! If you want to be rescued, you'll have to cooperate. I don't want to get bit!"

He stopped growling and stared at me, cocking his head to one side. So I talked to him some more, very soft and friendly sounding. "Here, boy! Come on, come over here!"

"How can he see through all that hair?" Paul wanted to know. "Are you sure it's him? The right dog?"

"It's him. We saw his picture. He looks like he's been dragged through the mud and the brambles, but it's him. Here, boy! I'm not that nasty old Mr. Royce or Spud. Come on, boy!"

I guess he decided to trust me. He trotted toward us and looked up. His shaggy tail gave a tentative wag.

"I'll have to go in after him," I said and swung my leg over the window frame.

Just as I picked him up I heard C.B. doing her whippoorwill call. Paul turned off the flashlight and we froze, as if we were playing statues. Only this was for real. If they caught us again, they'd know darned well what we were there for. Though we hadn't seen any sign of a gun, there was a whole lake out there they could drown us in. I didn't have any doubt that they'd think of something to keep us quiet.

We heard the murmur of voices, and then the car door opened and slammed shut again. "Shall we take the rest of the groceries with us?" Spud asked. "Must be fifteen-twenty dollars worth left."

"What's fifteen-twenty dollars when we get the ransom money?" Royce asked. I could smell his cigarette, real strong; he was close to the front of the shed. What if they were ready to come in and get MacDuff now, to take him home?

I stared at the black hole that was the window, knowing there was no way I'd ever get out through it without being heard. I was holding MacDuff against my chest, and I could feel his heart beating against my hand.

"Not much," Spud agreed. "On the other hand, some of that stuff might lead the cops to us. I mean, that cheap brand of caviar you like, there's some of that left. And your brother-in-law knows you eat the stuff; if the cops ask questions in the right places, that caviar could lead right to us. He wouldn't cover for you, would he?"

Royce made a snorting sound. "Tim Hagen? That would be the day! He can't stand me any better'n I can stand him! All right, let's take the groceries. What about the dog food? It's practically all still left, fussy little mutt never ate any of it. I expected he'd be spoiled rotten, but he wouldn't even touch the caviar!"

Spud laughed. It was an odd sound, not fun to hear. "He's probably used to a more expensive brand! Yeah, we better take the dog food, too. In case that clerk remembers selling us a lot of that kind. Maybe we'll be lucky and the old gal won't ever report anything to the cops. Your brother-in-law said she hates publicity, didn't he?"

"Yeah." Another car door slammed. They must be loading all their stuff, ready to leave. "All he talks about is Mrs. Trentwood this, Mrs. Trentwood that! Anybody silly enough to pay out a fortune to get a stupid little dog back, she can't be so bright!"

Spud laughed again. "Lucky for us anyway. And lucky your brother-in-law talked about how goofy she is over the dog. Otherwise we'd never have had the idea, would we? Come on. Let's get the last of it and get out of here."

"You think we ought to check and see if the mutt is still in there?"

"He's still in there, I heard him when we locked up those fool kids. I'm not gonna open that door again, not for anything. He's too quick. If I'd known how many times he'd get away on us, I probably wouldn't have snatched him in the first place."

Royce sounded sour. "Think how much worse it

would have been if we'd had to kidnap the other one! Nearly wrecked that house, trying to get his little royal highness out of there without the big one coming along, too."

"Yeah, well—" It sounded as if Spud had his head inside the car, and then his voice became louder again. "Could have been worse, if he'd decided you were a crook instead of just playing a game. Can you imagine what it would be like, having those teeth fasten on your leg?"

Royce said something surly, but they were walking away now and I couldn't understand what it was. What about Leroy? Had they done something to him? Where was he?

MacDuff whimpered, and I realized I was squeezing him too tight. "Sorry, fella," I whispered and started edging toward the window. I hoped I could get out without having to turn the light on again; if those thugs were going back and forth between the car and the cottage, it was too dangerous to use the flashlight.

"Danny?" Paul hissed at me. "You coming?"

"Yeah. Here, take the dog and I'll climb out." I handed over MacDuff, who didn't seem to mind, and I had one leg over the windowsill when we heard them coming back. For a minute I teetered there, nearly falling off first inside and then outside the building. I heard the woodpile shift under Paul's feet and knew it would make more noise if I came down on it, so I stayed where I was.

Royce and Spud weren't trying to be especially quiet. They threw more stuff into the station wagon, and Royce stood for a minute at the opposite end of the shed from me, coughing and swearing about it.

"You gotta quit smoking those things," Spud said finally. "What do you want to do about those kids? We going to come back and turn 'em loose, afterward?"

"You crazy? And have 'em describe us to everybody in the county? That one kid is a real blabber-mouth, didn't you see that stuff in the paper about him?"

"Well, somebody's going to come and find 'em sooner or later. Or did you intend—?"

It was pretty uncomfortable straddling that windowsill, especially since the window was small and I had to hunch forward. Still, it was better than being locked in that garage, if I was getting the right drift on what they were saying.

"Kids monkeying around in old buildings, accidents happen," Royce said. He coughed again. "Lots of hay in there, kids playing with matches, you never know what'll happen. Place could go up in smoke in just a few minutes."

For a few seconds I forgot to breathe. Boy, these guys were really something!

"A fire might be seen from town," Spud said after

a minute. Not like he cared about us or anything.

"So? Late as it is, probably nobody in this two-bit town is still up. But if they do see it, it'll attract attention on the opposite side of the lake from where we're going to be. Come on, we're ready, aren't we? Let's get out of here. You wiped off everything we'd touched in there, didn't you?"

"I already told you. They won't find any fingerprints. OK, let's go get the money and then get out of here. You think we ought to pour gas on something on the end of the garage?"

"And have the cops looking for an arsonist?" Royce demanded in disgust. "Don't be a fool; they can tell if a fire's been set with something like gas. Nah, dry as it is and that hay in there, it'll burn easy."

"Be better if we could figure something to set it off after we've got a few minutes head start. How about, one of those candles we found in the kitchen? Put it in some hay up against the doors, so it'll start a fire when it burns down. Whatta you think?"

Talk about cold-blooded, I thought. As soon as they started moving toward the cottage again, I slid over the sill, nearly fell on the shifting firewood, and stumbled into the woods. Paul touched me and whispered in my ear.

"You think we'd better stick around and try to keep the garage from burning? Or shall we get the heck out of here right now?"

Our eyes were beginning to adjust to the darkness, now. I saw C.B. before I heard her. "Let's draw straws to see who stays to put out the candle when they're gone. The other two of us will take MacDuff and hightail it along the beach for help."

I hardly recognized my own voice. "Don't waste time drawing straws. You two go. I'll catch up with you. If I don't, get to Gramps. He's pretty good for an adult, he won't waste a lot of time with questions. Go on, before they come out again!"

I don't mind admitting I was scared, crouching there in the edge of the trees waiting for Royce and Spud to leave. It seemed to me it took them a long time, although I suppose really it wasn't more than five minutes. I couldn't see what they were doing, and they didn't talk much anymore.

When the motor roared in the station wagon, I flattened on the ground, smelling the dry pine needles under my face, until they had backed out onto the road.

I hardly remember running around the end of the shed and to the garage.

There was the candle, a little short one stuck into a can lid, with loose hay around it, right up against the garage door. They hadn't noticed that their improvised lock had been opened or they might have looked around for us.

I put out the candle, then opened the garage, just

in case we'd somehow missed something. "Leroy? Leroy, you around anywhere?" I called softly, but there was no answering sound. By now I didn't doubt they'd have finished Leroy off if he bothered them, and it sounded like he had.

There wasn't any time to think about that, though. The important thing was to notify the sheriff and try to catch the kidnappers before they got away with the ransom money.

I didn't catch up with C.B. and Paul until they were nearly home. They'd gone past the Hopes'— C.B. knew her folks would want to know everything that had happened before they'd get around to calling the sheriff—and everybody but MacDuff was puffing when we went up our back steps. MacDuff seemed to think it was all an entertainment put on just for his benefit. I guess it was nice somebody was enjoying it, but I was so worried about Leroy I could hardly stand it.

Gramps was home, just getting out of the car. MacDuff raced up to him, barking, and Gramps turned around and said, "What the heck—? Where'd you come from—Danny, that you?"

For a grown-up, Gramps was really neat. He didn't make us waste any time filling him in on anything but the essentials. He took one look at us and led the way into the house. He called Ben Newton himself.

"Charlie Minden here, Ben. My grandson and his

friends just rescued a kidnapped dog, and if we hurry maybe we can catch the kidnappers when they go to pick up the ransom. Haven't been drinking a thing, Ben, cross my heart. It's Mrs. Trentwood's little dog, what's his name? MacDuff? You can call her and tell her he's been rescued, she'll verify he was kidnapped. She was to put the money in a deserted mailbox out beyond the Lodge . . . whose mailbox?"

"Patrick's," C.B. supplied when my memory failed.

"Patrick's mailbox," Gramps said into the phone. "They're supposed to pick up the money after midnight. It's nearly that now. We'll meet you out there." He hung up before the sheriff could ask any more questions.

"Fastest way to get there," Gramps said, "would be across the lake. Jerry Fowler's got a nice little outboard; he'll let us use it when we tell him it's an emergency."

So we all tore over to the Fowlers. The phone rang behind us, but Gramps didn't pause. "No sense answering that. It's bound to be the sheriff, and he knows where we're going. Come on."

The Fowlers were in bed, but that didn't stop Gramps. He pounded on the door and when Mr. Fowler came out wearing red and white striped pajama bottoms, Gramps didn't waste words.

"Emergency. Have to get over to the Lodge as fast as possible; we need your boat."

For a few seconds Mr. Fowler teetered there in his bare feet, then closed his mouth. "Sure. Help yourself."

He was still standing there looking after us when Gramps revved up the outboard, and we took off across the lake. All four of us, plus MacDuff.

I wondered if MacDuff knew where we were going. Because he seemed excited, now; I was sitting in the bow, and he stood on his hind legs, leaning against me, his floppy ears blowing back from his head.

The outboard was loud in the night as we skimmed across the water. "We may scare them off," Paul suggested.

"We'll land a good distance from the mailbox," Gramps shouted back. "And those fellers will be in a car, they won't hear our motor over their own."

I hoped he was right. I wanted to catch them, and I wanted to get Mrs. Trentwood's money back for her. But most of all I wanted to know where Leroy was. I wanted to know if he was all right.

It was startling when Gramps cut the motor and we drifted toward shore. The quiet was unbelievable. I guess the people who lived around there were used to outboard motors, because even as late as it was, nobody came out to investigate.

Except Mrs. Trentwood.

She stood there in the doorway of the Lodge looking toward her own dock until we called out to her.

When she was sure who it was, she came running across the beach. I lifted MacDuff and jumped out into the water with him; he was squirming so hard it was all I could do to get him to land before I dropped him.

He bounded across the sand, and I heard Mrs. Trentwood's cry before his excited barking drowned her out.

"The sheriff called, but I couldn't believe it until I saw him," she said. She hugged MacDuff, dirty as he was, and he licked joyfully at her face. "Did you find your dog, too, Danny?"

"No. Not yet," I said, and it was hard to keep my voice from cracking. "Is the sheriff here yet?"

"No," she said, but a minute later Ben Newton materialized out of the shadows. He was in uniform, and he was wearing a gun.

"Couldn't you have made a little more noise, Charlie?" he asked Gramps. "Everybody in the county must know you came across the lake."

"City slickers don't know the difference. We going to catch them picking up the money, Ben?"

"I hope so. I called my deputy, but I had to leave a message for him. He wasn't home yet. So what I'm going to have to do is—" He looked over the bunch of us, there in the light from the Lodge. "I'm going to have to deputize all of you until he gets here. And you're going to follow my orders exactly, you understand? No grandstand heroics, nothing like that. Just follow orders."

"Deputize us?" Paul echoed. "Us kids, too?"

"Hold up your right hands and repeat after me—"

It was sort of unreal, repeating the words he said. Everybody but Mrs. Trentwood; he told Gramps later he left her out because he didn't think she'd be much use.

"I don't have any badges for you, but that doesn't make it any less official," the sheriff told us. "You, Charlie," he said to Gramps, "are going to help me set up a roadblock in front of the Lodge until my deputy gets here. I've already talked to Hagen; he's watching the road to see if they go by."

My mouth was dry. "What do you want us to do, sheriff?"

He looked at us. "Just stay out of trouble," he said. "We've got enough of that already. Come on, Charlie."

We kids all stared at one another while the grown-ups headed back toward the Lodge.

"It's not fair," C.B. said. "After he deputized us! What was that for?"

"So he could give us orders," Paul said. I could tell he was as disappointed as I was.

"But he didn't give us any," I pointed out.

"So what good are we as deputies?" Paul wanted to know. "I don't think much of his sense of humor, if that's what it was."

"He didn't say we had to stay here," I added. "He didn't say we couldn't go along the beach and up through the woods and watch the mailbox to see if Royce and Spud come to get the money. If we hurry, we might beat them there."

C.B. started to giggle. "I'll bet we will. They probably had to stop to fix a tire."

"How do you know that?"

"Paul loosened the valve cores on the back two tires. I'll bet they either fell off when the car got moving, or they had at least one leak before they went very far. We hope."

"Hey!" I didn't trouble to hide my admiration. "That was quick thinking!"

"Your idea about watching the mailbox is OK, too," Paul said. "Come on, let's go!"

I guess we all knew Ben Newton wouldn't approve of us going up to the mailbox. But he hadn't said we *couldn't* go; and it was a dirty trick, making us deputies and then leaving us out of everything.

I'd have said I was too tired to run anymore, but we all had our second wind by then. We took off down the beach. There was enough moonlight so we could see pretty well until we had to leave the lake.

It was slower going through the woods, but the path was one that must have been used a lot; it was wide enough and firm enough so that we could walk fast, even in the dark. When we finally burst out of the trees at the road, we were all panting so loud it was a good thing there was nobody there. They'd have heard us for sure.

"How do we know they haven't already been here?" C.B. puffed.

"We could look in the mailbox and see if the money's there." I was glad Paul was breathing the same way I was.

"No," I said quickly. "The sheriff said to stay out of trouble. We'd really mess everything up if the car came and we were there at the mailbox."

We picked the best location to see from and flopped down on our stomachs in the grass. The moon made the shadows an even deeper black. There was a tight knot in my middle. We lay still and concentrated on slowing our breathing. I tried not to think what they might have done to Leroy if he'd interfered with their plans.

If they hadn't done anything to him, why hadn't he come home by this time? Resolutely, I pushed the idea away.

And then we heard the car coming.

We heard it before we saw the headlights. We crouched in the grass, ready to spring up and run if we had to.

The car came slowly toward us, the headlights picking out the group of decrepit mailboxes.

The moonlight didn't do much good now because we were sort of blinded by the headlights; we were looking right into them. We didn't see the door open, but when Spud stepped out we did see *him*. Clearly, in their own headlights, as he opened the mailbox and scooped out something and then disappeared back into the car.

Royce was driving, and he gunned it as soon as Spud was inside. They turned around in the next driveway, and when their back-up lights came on we could see the license plate as plain as anything.

"FCD 523," C.B. breathed, and Paul and I repeated it to ourselves to commit it to memory. "FCD 523." It was like a poem.

And then the car accelerated and was gone in the direction of town.

For a few seconds we lay in the grass, still repeating the license number, and then everybody took a deep breath, all at the same time.

"Do we go back by the road?" C.B. asked, and I knew she was feeling as weak in the stomach and knees as I was.

"It's the shortest way, so let's go," I said.

We didn't run back. We were too tired. We kept listening for some shooting, but there wasn't anything like that.

When we came around the final curve in the road, there were all the cars, all over the road. The sheriff's car, with flashing lights on the top of it, and the deputy's car, with more lights, and a couple of other vehicles the deputy must have rounded up. And there were Spud and Royce, standing in front of their station wagon, and they didn't look very dangerous now. All the starch had gone right out of them.

They couldn't drive through the blockade of cars, and there was nowhere else to go. They'd had to stop. When they did, a line of armed men met them.

It was all over.

I think Mrs. Trentwood was so glad to have Mac-Duff back that she didn't really care all that much about the money. The sheriff said he had to keep it for evidence for the time being, anyway.

"Wow!" Paul said. His eyes were shining in the revolving colored lights. "Nobody's going to believe this! I forgot all about the guys waiting for me to come back with the bowling trophy. I wonder if they've all gone home?"

"Well, you got it, and witnesses to say you actually went to the Miller place. So you ought to pass your initiation and become a member of the Secret Club," I said.

"Yeah. That's right." He looked at me quite differently from the way he had when he'd come home with Aunt Mattie for dinner. "I was thinking . . . I'll sponsor you for membership if you want to join, Danny. I don't know if you'll even have to do an initiation trick—what you did tonight was a lot scarier than crawling into an empty house and snitching a trophy."

I shrugged. "Yeah, I guess. If it's a fun club."

"It is," Paul assured me. "I'll ask the guys, OK?"

Spud and Royce were loaded into the deputy's car, in the back seat where there are no door handles so the passengers can't get out, and behind a wire mesh. The sheriff and Gramps came toward us, looking tired but satisfied. The other men got into their cars and headed for home.

"We saw 'em, Sheriff," Paul said. "Taking the money out of the mailbox! We recognized Spud in the headlights! And we got the license number, too! Will we have to go to court and testify at their trial?"

Ben Newton looked at us the way grown-ups do when they're deciding whether to hit you or not. "I thought I told you to stay out of trouble."

"We didn't get in any trouble. We hid in the grass," C.B. assured him. "They never knew we were there."

Gramps chuckled. "They got you there, Ben."

"I guess so," the sheriff admitted reluctantly. "But the next time you kids get mixed up in a kidnapping, or anything else that looks dangerous, call me in a little sooner, will you?"

We all agreed to that. I hoped I never got involved in anything criminal again as long as I lived.

Gramps dropped a hand on my shoulder. "Well, boy, we better get in Jerry Fowler's boat and head for home. C.B.'s coming with us, what about you, Paul?"

"Guess I'll hitch a ride with the sheriff," Paul said. "Maybe he'll explain to my folks what happened. They think I've been in bed asleep."

"Sheriff," I said, around the lump that had formed in my throat, "did they say anything about Leroy? I mean, he's missing."

"Leroy? That horse-sized dog? Forgot all about him." Ben Newton pushed back his hat and scratched his head. "I don't know how long I can live in the same town with the three of you, you and Charlie and Leroy, if you're all afflicted with that Minden Curse."

"Did they say where he is?" I waited, hoping—no, *praying*—that they hadn't shot him.

"They didn't say. But I know where he is. He's over there in the front seat of my car," Newton said.

"How in tarnation did he get there?" Gramps asked, and he was no more astonished than I was.

"He's just like the rest of you. If there's anything exciting going on, he shows up. How do you do it?" He didn't wait for an answer. "He looks a bit banged up, and he's pretty dirty. From the look of him I'd say he's been in the same place that pooch of Mrs. Trentwood's was. But he must have gotten loose. If he wanted out of a garage and those men were fool enough to open the door, I don't think they could hold him, big as he is."

"But where's he been?" Gramps demanded.

"I guess when he got loose he headed for home and didn't find anybody there. If he tried to track Danny down by following his trail, the poor dog must have had a merry chase, from the sound of things. Anyway, where I found him was at the Pepper place. Mrs. Pepper went over to the neighbors to borrow some fuses when her electricity went off. And while she was gone, the kids tried to light some candles, and they set the curtains afire. The kids panicked and didn't even know enough to get out of the house; the oldest one is only six, you know."

"Well, that dog of yours was passing by and heard the kids screaming. He made such a racket Mrs. Pepper came running, and the neighbors called the fire department, and by the time the adults got there old Leroy had dragged the littlest one out onto the porch. The firemen put the fire out all right, only damage was in the kitchen. Then everybody began making a fuss over the dog, so I guess he didn't bother to go on looking for Danny. They were feeding him milk and cookies when I got there. He's been in my car for hours. I didn't have time to take him home. I tried to call you back and tell you, but you'd left the house after you told me about the kidnapping."

I didn't wait to hear the rest of it. I ran toward the

patrol car and jerked open the door. Leroy met me with an enthusiastic slurp across the face. Which was maybe just as well, because I wouldn't have wanted anyone to think the moisture there was tears or anything like that.

When we roared back across the lake, waking up the residents of Indian Lake for the last time that night, Leroy was with me in the middle of the boat. He sat just like a person with his rump on the seat and his front legs on the bottom of the boat. Every once in a while he licked my ear.

Gramps cut the engine, and we coasted toward shore. Mr. and Mrs. Fowler were there to meet us, and Mr. and Mrs. Hope were there, too, all of them hastily dressed.

"Oh, oh," C.B. said in a small voice. "I should have gone home with the sheriff, too."

"We'll help you explain," Gramps told her. "We need the practice. Mattie will be home day after tomorrow."

Boy, I was tired, I thought. I couldn't wait to fall into bed, and I wouldn't even mind sharing it with Leroy.

If there was anything to this Minden Curse business, it promised to be an interesting winter.